NAUGHTY SPANKING ONE

A collection of twenty erotic stories

Edited by Miranda Forbes

Published by Accent Press Ltd – 2008
ISBN 9781906125837
Reprinted 2009

Printed in the UK by CPI Bookmarque, Croydon, CR0 4TD

Cover Design by
Red Dot Design

Xcite Books – always something new...

For more information about our books,
toys and movies please visit

www.xcitebooks.com

Contents

Rebound Guy
by Sommer Marsden

Perry is my rebound guy. He's basically around to help me get over Scott. Not a problem. I can hang in for a bit. It's good to have the company. The sex. A person to hang out with. I haven't told him outright that he's just a filler. I assume he knows. Six years of intense relationship does not disappear over night but a girl has needs. Perry is good in bed.

I put the finishing touches on the outfit and steel myself for the evening. I love spending time with Perry but most of his friends make me want to chew my own wrists open. Tonight we are going to a party throw by Don and Diana. I hate them for many reasons but the foremost are their names. The double D thing. Also, they talk too fucking much.

I am told the party is to celebrate some big event in their relationship. I couldn't give a hoot about their relationship. Or them. However, an appearance at the shindig guarantees two things: really good liquor as they go for only the best and, most importantly, I will get laid.

When I answer the doorbell, Perry does a quick scan of my ensemble and smiles.

"Nice. I like the skirt. You look gorgeous."

"Thank you," I laugh. Even in heels I have to stand on tiptoe to kiss him. I am not short. At nearly six feet tall, Perry towers over me a good five or six inches. He is tall and big all over and I like that. I like that he makes me feel small whereas with most men I can stare them straight in the eye even while barefoot. "Now, about this party," I say and light a cigarette.

Perry frowns at my smoke. He doesn't like it that I smoke. He really doesn't like that I smoke around him. But, like I said, he is the rebound guy. He'll just have to deal with it.

"We don't have to stay long, Erin," he sighs in response to my unasked question. "And must you smoke around me? Really?" His green eyes turn a little grey with what I can only assume is frustration. Maybe anger. Whatever.

"Sorry, I'm nervous," I say and wave the smoke away from him as best I can. "I can assume that as usual I will be stuffed with jumbo shrimp and premium vodka and regaled with tales of love in the world of marriage?" I grin to make sure he knows I am joking. Kind of.

"Probably. Now if you can crush that death stick out we can go on our way and get this over with." He puts his big arm around me and guides me out of the apartment. He locks my door and takes my arm. I let him do all this because I like it when a man is in charge and even though he isn't, I let him think he is for now.

On the way to the car, I light another cigarette and listen to him let out a low growl. I smile at him as I pass through a puddle of light that spills from the street lamp. "Don't you want to know what's under my skirt?" I ask both to tease him and to make sure he knows that I fully intend getting fucked by him tonight.

"Of course I do. But can I guess?" He unlocks the car, waits for me to crush out the smoke and sit. Then he shuts my door. Ever the gentleman. When he gets in the driver's side he raises his eyebrows and waits.

I notice how big his hands are on the steering wheel. I've never really noticed before. "Sure. Guess," I whisper as I study his broad palms, long, thick fingers and square shiny fingernails.

"Purple thong. The one with the little gold circle dead centre in the back. I love that triangle. I always try to see if I can fit the very tip of my tongue through the little hole."

I swallow hard and can hear a dry click in my throat. Will I even make it to the fucking party? I wonder. I shake my head like a dog shaking off water. "Nope. Try again."

He caresses the steering wheel and I think of his hands doing that to my skin. That and more. The soft sounds of his rough hands caressing my skin and then, in my mind, the sound of that huge hand delivering a first delicious blow on my ass cheek. I suck in a breath and he cocks his head and grins at me.

"The white one. Same panties, different colour."

"Nope." In my mind I can see his big fingers sliding into my pussy. Disappearing from view but doing secret magical things deep inside me where I can't see them. I shift in the leather seat and it gives a seductive sigh as I move.

"Hmm. Are they new? They must be. After a month, I am usually very good at this game."

I nod. He gets a point. "They are. They are new."

Perry moves his hand to my thigh and heat flows up my thigh into my chest straight to my throat. I can feel my chest blushing crimson the way it does when I get horny. A scarlet stain of desire that I refuse to be ashamed of. "Let's see them," he whispers and leans in to kiss the hot blush on my skin. Just so I know he sees it, I assume.

I sigh and it sounds loud in the quiet of the closed car. "Okay, but then we go. The sooner we go, the sooner we can leave," I say, exercising my control. I turn to the side and raise my ass. He lifts my skirt almost daintily. As if it is made of vintage lace instead of soft, faded denim.

When he laughs, I smile out the window. He thinks it's funny. I think it's funny that he most likely assumes it's a joke. Sex with Perry is good but vanilla. Hot but generic. I always come but none of my kinks show up to play. I don't know if it's that I don't trust him yet or that I don't trust myself. Perhaps I am not ready to bare all to someone else after a six-year relationship.

He reads it aloud and I let him. "*Spank Me*. Nice. So, you want people to spank you, Erin?"

"Only those who read my panties," I joke but a shiver runs

3

through me as I say it. In some small way I have let him in on a secret. One I doubt he had figured out. One part of me wants him to know and another part of me fears him knowing.

"Ready?" Perry asks as he smoothes a big hand over my bottom. Then without waiting for my answer he starts the car.

We are off to Don and Diana's place. The excitement is overwhelming. OK, so I'm lying.

I relinquish my coat and accept a vodka with a twist when we enter. The place is full of beautiful people in expensive clothes sipping booze that costs more than my rent. I sip too. I play along. I sink into the false security of being around people who have way more money than I can even dream of. That is fine. Money isn't everything. When I feel overwhelmed, I imagine them going to bed every night in their satin pajamas and having sex in the missionary position. Not everything can be slapped with a price tag. When was the last time Don had spanked Diana until her cheeks were the colour of ripe summer cherries? How many times had she relished the hot welted skin of her bottom that proved that he owned her? How many times had he braced herself on hands and knees while he fucked her up the ass until she screamed? How many times had he given her twenty lashes with a whip? I had to smile just trying to imagine it. I would take my priceless orgasms over their pricey booze any day.

I walk into the next room and hear Perry's deep, comfortable voice. "Erin works for a rehab company. She prepares resumés and assists on job searches for people who have been injured in their current occupations." It sounds like he's bragging but I realize how very boring it sounds. Yes, it sounds boring but it really isn't. I smile at him and he smiles back.

I finally get him alone and I sip my vodka and whisper, "So, this big thing in Don and Diana's relationship … what is it? Renewing the vows? Baby? They learned to do it doggy style?" I ask and laugh. "I'm sorry. That was rude."

He doesn't frown, though. He just brushes my long dark locks out of my face and kisses my nose. "No. They have

4

switched over to an open marriage. This is a coming out party, so to speak."

I feel my mouth open and close. I feel my cheeks heat and my chest flush again. Don and Diana? An open marriage? It had to be a fucking joke. Those two? The straightest of straight, the plainest of vanilla. Perry is laughing and I feel like I can't breathe.

"Joking," I say, "you are joking." He must be. It is the only explanation.

But Perry shakes his head and his almost black hair sways with the movement. I notice that here and there is a touch of silver. Just enough to make my new panties moist at the crotch. For the second time, I notice how very big and compelling his hands are.

I glance into the corner and see Don kissing a blonde. She is not Diana. She is tall and willowy. The back of her red dress barely hides the swell of her ass. Barely contains her ass crack. I swallow and my heart beats an erratic drunken rhythm.

"How about those panties?" Perry asks and I blink at him. I stare at him and wonder if somehow I got drunk and didn't notice.

"What?"

"I think that would certainly liven things up, don't you?" he asks and his hand when it touches my wrist is cold from holding his drink.

"My panties?" I say dumbly, unable to process that this man that I have written off is now provoking my very own kinks.

"Yes. *Spank me*. It says so right on them. White cotton bikinis, size medium according to the tag. It's an invitation, or am I mistaken?"

"What?" I sound stupid. I feel stupid. But my body is not and it is reacting to the information it is processing. My pussy has grown slick, my nipples have peaked and are attentive. My face feels like it is on fire and my breathing has gone shallow like I might pass out.

"Everyone!" He is no longer addressing me. He is now

5

addressing the room. My head goes light as my cunt goes tight. "I think we have a lovely way to celebrate Don and Diana's new outlook on marriage. I have a special treat for you all!"

Half sideshow barker, half Baptist minister, he addresses the small gathering. "Perry!" I hiss. "Perry!"

He ignores me.

Perry takes my hand and I follow. I follow blindly, mutely, dumbly. I follow because part of me craves this more than anything. He sits on a celery-coloured settee and pulls me down next to him. "I propose a sound thrashing for my lovely companion. Her name is Erin. We've been dating for about a month now. I am the rebound guy."

The crowd chuckles in unison. Some of them tsk with disapproval but Perry raises his palms to calm them. He nods and smiles as if to say, *It's okay, I understand.* I feel my face grow hotter. Any hotter and I might lose consciousness. I bow my head both embarrassed and excited all at once.

"No, no, don't be that way," he goes on. "Erin is wearing very special panties and I would like to share them … share her with all of you. For tonight. In honour of Don and Diana."

I could leave. I know it. I could get up, slap his face, walk out. I do not. I wait.

Perry pats his lap and I stare for a moment. I breathe for several beats and weigh my options. The itching, creeping yearning is bigger than my pride and I hit the floor with my knees, bow my torso over his lap. I wait.

"Very good, Erin," he say slowly. "I wondered if you would or wouldn't." With that he flips up the back of my denim skirt and bares my white cotton panties with the hot pink words to the room. A low murmur sweeps through the gathering and he waits.

Quiet descends and he hooks his fingers into my waistband and pulls my panties down. The air and the stares and the wonder are as palpable to my bare skin as his blows will be. "Lovely, isn't she?" Perry says, addressing the crowd. "Are you up for ten?" he asks, now addressing me.

My stomach flutters and my knees shake. I feel a slow slickness grow between my thighs, slipping down the insides of my legs like water. My cunt flickers and clutches and flits. I squirm a little on his knees and my nipples pinch under my silk bra. I nod, not trusting my voice.

"I invite you all to count with me!" Perry barks and another murmur ripples through the room.

The first blow lands and my head flies back. I want him to fuck me right then and there. If not him, someone. Any man in the room that comes with a cock attached will do. His big palm blazes a trail on my pale skin and I cry out in pain and in excitement.

The blows rain down and with each the crowd gets louder. By the time they say five in unison, the sound of them hurts my ears. I see Diana in the corner. Her brown eyes wide, pupils dilated, cheeks flushed. She is shifting in place. She is wet and horny and ready under her plain blue dress. I know because I have worn that look before. I, however, do not need to worry about decorum because I am writhing on Perry's lap like a dog in heat.

We are up to eight and when he smoothes his hands over my ass, his fingers brush the seam of my sex. Tease around my clit. Hint at slipping deep inside me and bringing me all the way up to the peak where I want to be. I bite my tongue and focus on breathing. Two more to go and then I can see where it is he wants to go.

"Nine!" the crowd sings out in an overwhelmingly loud voice. I buck and squirm and wonder how red my ass is. How many welts I have. How my pussy looks, swollen and wet and bare to the men who are behind me. I wonder how many of them will masturbate or fuck their wives tonight picturing my tortured ass and my dripping cunt.

"TEN!" The sound is like a summer storm that has been contained in a single room. A crack and roar made up of excited voices and sexual energy.

I go limp on Perry's lap. I let the tears fall even as I relish the searing heat on my skin and the echoes of that heat deep

7

inside me where I am wet and ready.

Perry bends and pulls up my panties, smoothes my skirt. Then he whispers, "Let's go."

I nod. I rise. I stand tall and proud as if I have just delivered a speech. Not at all like a woman who has been spanked in front of a room full of near strangers. Both Don and Diana hug me and whisper, "thank you" in my ear.

I might have been wrong about them.

Out on the street, on the way to the car, Perry runs his hand over my ass. Even through the denim it stings. I wince but I grow wetter still under my panties. I want him. I want him to fuck me. With his fingers, with his cock, with his tongue. Whatever he wants, however he wants, I want it too.

"I took a chance," he laughs. He opens the car and kisses my nose. "I know I'm just the rebound guy."

His eyes are large and sincere. Only a hint of his authority shines through. It is a statement not a question. No self-pity, just a fact.

I stare back. Remember the sting and the power and the control he has just wielded over me. I smile, let my hand sit on the thumping heat of my skin. I imagine what we will do when we get home. "Yeah, I'm not so sure about that," I say and slide onto the leather seat and let him shut the door.

The Ice Queen Cometh
by Astarte

I knew it would end just as I had hoped. And from the slow, smouldering 'Grace Kelly' look that Marijka Bernstrøm gave me when I accepted her invitation to stay on with her in Nice, I knew that she knew that I knew!

There had been an unspoken sexual chemistry between us from the moment her Nordic-blue eyes locked with mine over her office desk in Chelsea, when she hired me six months ago. I was to handle press and public relations for London's 'Ice Queen of Fashion', as Vogue had dubbed this liberated blonde with stunning Scandinavian looks. This entailed promotion for her *FeminaFashion* label sold in High Street stores across the country, together with her exclusive *Marijka* label selling in her own London speciality boutiques for petite women like me, which she had recently opened in Knightsbridge and Mayfair. And, of course, I was to obtain as much media exposure as possible for the 'Ice Queen' herself, while filtering out the more lurid esoteric details of her exotic personal lifestyle as a Lipstick Dyke Domina that so fascinated the tabloid gossip-mongers and papparazzi.

Marijka had joined me on a weekend location shoot on the Cote d'Azur where I had arranged to photograph a selection from her Boutique Collection for one of the fashion glossies against the colourful floral background of the celebrated Nice Carnival.

It was an exhausting photo-shoot. I had to cope with

9

fractious models and a fractious fashion editor, a missing crate of dresses, a bloody-minded cameraman and a temperamental Carnival organizer. By the time I had wrapped it up on Sunday night and packed crew and crate back to London, I was as tense as a whore in church, emotionally drained and near to tears.

The 'Ice Queen', whose own pint-sized 5' 1", size 6 body, packing a 32D 'pair', does spectacular justice to the clothes she designs and wears with her celebrated and oft-photographed cool panache, had mercifully stayed aloof from these proceedings, allowing full rein to my overstretched organizational abilities. Now she stepped in with an invitation that was to change our lives.

She gave me one of her smouldering 'Grace Kelly' looks that got me hot, discombobulated and wobbly-kneed.

"You need therapeutic pampering after such a stressful weekend, my dear! Some disciplined massage, perhaps? You shall be my guest at the Hotel Negresco! I have booked us into their luxury Louis XIV suite for two nights and you can accompany me back to London on Wednesday's evening flight."

She focused that look on me again, deadly as a laser beam.

"We shall be very *very* comfortable together and you will find my massage has a soothing bite."

It was an invitation brooking no refusal; a summons delivered with dark depths of hidden meaning and sensual promise. Marijka gift-wrapped her command with a regal smile as she took my hand, her ice-blue eyes devouring me and coveting the curves of my tits and arse like a Siamese cat eyeing a saucer of cream.

Ice can burn! I blushed at her icy-hot gaze, feeling my body tingle and my clit throb in anticipation of the 'afterglow' pussyplay that would follow the sort of stinging therapy the 'Ice Queen' was rumoured to dispense to her chosen few.

As a single and successful career girl in PR, I have assiduously cultivated a no-nonsense veneer to my 'femme' personality, but beneath that façade I am a submissive softie

10

who craves the imperious attentions and intimate caring control of a strict Domina. The thought of Marijka Heart-throb undressing me to bare my shapely derrière and subjecting my dimpled cheeks to the discipline of a hard spanking brought a wetness to my crotch and a flutter to my breast.

Marijka had been the Domina of my lonely fantasies ever since she hired me. Had I found my longed-for conquisita? Could I melt this Scandinavian 'Ice Queen' between my thighs? There was only one way to find out. I accepted her offer! I can't do *femme fatale* smouldering looks, but my glowing eyes and flushed face betrayed me. She knew I would give her my body in total wanton submission to her sensual demands and pleasure.

On Monday morning I cancelled my cheap return flight, checked out of my modest two-star back-street *pension* and moved in with Marijka at the grandiose Negresco on the Promenade des Anglais; the finest, most luxurious hotel on the French Riviera.

If you wish to be dommed and disciplined as a prelude to pussyplay by a seductive 'Grace Kelly' look-alike, the Negresco's opulent Louis XIV suite, with its majestically canopied bed and strategically placed mirrors, is as good as it gets when it comes to a suitably decadent venue. It proved an appropriately opulent setting for Marijka Bernstrøm to seduce and take Adele Adams, her petite submissive English-rose Press Officer, to her bed and breast on that fateful Monday night!

But Marijka was not to be rushed into shaking Eve's Tree. Adams had to wait for her promised apple!

"We have the night before us, Adele, dearest! First we shall soak our gorgeous gams in a warm, perfumed bath and then buzz our 'Brazilians' together! Afterwards we shall enjoy a candlelit dinner *a deux* at an intimate little restaurant I know in the Old Town, run by Chantal and her gorgeous girlfriend. I shall give your darling derrière its well-deserved 'massage' later."

The look and the lick that came with her promise twanged

my sexual antenna to a vibrant thrum!

It was nearly midnight before we parted company with Chantal at her restaurant 'Le Chat Gourmand' and we paused for a nightcap on the way back at the 'Sappho Bar', another of Marijka's intimate little hideaways-for-girls in Nice's old town.

As Marijka intended, I was dreamily relaxed, but feeling hot and wet with anticipation for her touch, when she finally closed the door to our luxurious suite, kicked the killer heels off her dainty feet and led me by the hand into the mirrored bedroom.

"It's time to unwrap my present!" she whispered with a throaty giggle, and turned to undress me. Her breath was warm on my neck as she unzipped my dress and peeled it off. I was wearing a white, satin-panelled, open-bottom girdle that I hoped effectively accentuated my more positive attributes, while concealing less desired figure-faults within in its moulding embrace. It, and the six taut suspenders holding my white lace-topped stockings, framed my naughty bits; brazen Brazilian and dimpled derrière! At this moment I felt like a 'Virgin Bride'!

Marijka stood back to admire the view, smiled and smouldered with silent approval of all she surveyed – rich cream for the Pussycat! She freed my heavy breasts from their constraint to expose their firm beauty, (I'm very proud of my perfect 34D tits). I tweaked my nipples to excited erection and presented them to her in wanton surrender.

"Adele, my darling!" she breathed, as she moved to sample the goods. She cupped their warmth appreciatively, bending to suck at the luscious fruit I was offering her 'On Special!'

"Undress me!"

I hastened to obey my Viking plunderer, disrobing her of her shimmering ice-blue wrap-around Mylar blouse with a plunging neckline that exposed rather than concealed her bra-less, firmly contoured 32Ds. She had nipples as large and dangerous as icebergs! Their hard points tempted my lips with their taunting arousal. I fondled them briefly on my way south,

12

my hands lingering to caress the lissom lines of her back and buttocks. I knelt at her feet. My face nuzzled the lips of her silky-smooth Venus in submissive adoration as I undid her suspender belt and slowly peeled down the Dita von Teeze stockings from her shapely legs. She stepped out of them, turned and pulled the bed's richly brocaded coverlet back to sit down on the soft Egyptian cotton sheets, positioning herself strategically to admire her reflection in the giant wall mirror.

She patted her thighs in silent command. London's 'Ice Queen of Fashion' was about to transform her Press Officer's submissive fantasies into painfully blissful reality.

She placed me across her bare thighs, forcing me to arch my back, the better to display my dimpled pink cheeks and expose my pouting pussy to her gaze and to the mirror's reflection. It was a deliciously humiliating and helpless pose.

"You, my *elskling*, are a flirtatious *slata*. The look you gave Chantal in her restaurant was positively lascivious and I will not tolerate such lewd slutmanners from my pretty Press Officer. I am about to smack your very naughty bottom!"

She caressed my bared warmth beneath her hand, speculatively kneading and pinching the soft cheeks exposed so helplessly to her gaze, before running a fingernail along the crack of my cuntlips. Her touch was like an electric shock; a thrilling jolt of pure ecstasy. I moaned and wriggled, desperate now for the heat of her spanking hand and that liberating catharsis of pain I so desired.

"Yes, Mistress!" I cooed. I wiggled my butt provocatively, narcissistically worshipping our joint reflections in the giant mirror.

"Naughty Press Officers deserve to have their bottoms smacked! I shall have to give you a proper bare-bottomed spanking that you will not soon forget!"

She began to spank me. She slapped each bouncy cheek alternately in methodical rhythm, covering every inch from the dimple at the base of my spine to the sweet spot where soft thigh meets rounded cheek. I moaned, dreamily at first. Tears began to flow as the stinging strokes turned my cheeks from

13

warm rosy glow to a fiery furnace of heated flesh beneath the hard impact of her hand. She thrust her knee against my rapidly moistening cunt as she ratcheted up the severity of her blows, spreading the heated crimson blush across my quivering globes. My cheeks bounced erotically in the mirror's reflection, blushing to the beat of her hand, taking on an ever deepening crimson hue beneath the onslaught. I watched her raise her arm to deliver each stinging slap, swinging her ripe breasts into full reflected view each time she struck.

I squirmed and wriggled beneath her hand of love, rubbing my belly lasciviously against my Domina's bare knees. I felt the onset of a flowing wetness as my 'Ice Queen' brought me ever closer to the ecstatic release that would bond my pain to her pleasure.

Suddenly the blows ceased. I felt a hand caress between the cleft of my now burning cheeks. She gently parted them to explore the glistening jewel within my pussy. Her moistened finger sought the pink bud of my button, tarried a moment to rim the twitching flower, before sliding lower to the aroused wetness of my open love-labia, now swollen in plump sensuality. I squirmed appreciatively, arching my back to entice the welcome visitor to enter my portal, explore and stay awhile within its tight embrace. The wandering finger felt for my hooded pearl, coaxed it from its hiding place, rubbed it gently to excited hardness, before delving deep into the dark, juicy, cuntgrip of my vagina. Two fingers began to move sensuously in and out, bringing a soft mew of pleasure from my lips. I could feel glistening trails of cumjuice trickle down my inner thighs onto her knees. I bucked my hips to the slippery, oscillating rhythm of the most sensual frigging of my life!!

I could finally stand it no longer.

"Turn me over, my darling 'Ice Queen'! Take me! Fuck me!"

I struggled against Marijka's hold while squirming to suck her fingers ever deeper into the quicksand of my cunt.

"How dare you!"

My Domina pressed down firmly on the small of my back and removed her questing fingers from their sensual exploration.

"How dare you attempt to change position while I discipline you. For that, I shall punish you further."

A veritable hail of blows descended once more on my poor tortured bottom. My squeals of pleasure quickly turned to tears of anguish. My entire world shrank to nothing but the burning fire consuming my defenceless cheeks beneath that hail of stinging blows. Torment and ecstasy became one in the sweetness of pain.

I came!

At last, after what seemed an age, the metronome-like blows ceased. I lay in a limp, near-comatose state on a post-orgasmic plateau of euphoria while my dear disciplinarian caressed my bruised and reddened globes, absorbing the heat emanating from my punished flesh.

Marijka's hand began to unfasten the suspenders of my stockings to gently caress the back of my thighs.

"Your spanking is over and you've come all over my knee, you slurpy little slut! Get up! Kick off your heels! Slowly strip for me, starting with your stockings! Slip out of that girdle and flash me some flesh!"

I undressed obediently before Marijka's lingering appraisal, cupping my breasts at her and posing provocatively before the mirror. If she wanted me to play the slut, I would play! A hidden harlot lives imprisoned within me, like a genie waiting to be freed from a bottle. Marijka accepted my sluttish invitation to play, unleashing that wanton genie. She ran her sensuous fingers lasciviously over my breasts and hard nipples, lingering to tweak them before continuing down my body to caress my belly and heated bottom. The hard hand that had so cruelly spanked me, now glided delicately up my inner thighs to caress my dripping, swollen lovelips. My Domina bent forward to lick my Venus, her serpentine tongue flicking my sweetness, relishing the delicate flavour of my orgasmic juices and savouring the bouquet like a connoisseur sampling a fine wine.

"Adele, my delectable English rose! I have plucked your flower! Now I am Mistress of your body! I claim it as my prize in perpetuity!"

She pulled me roughly onto her and rolled over, pinning me beneath her.

"Now I plunder my treasure!"

My breathless retort, "Yes please, Mistress!" was smothered by a demanding kiss. Our tongues entwined. The 'Ice Queen' slipped smoothly between my open legs and began to grind against me, breast to breast, cunt to cunt. She grabbed a hot handful of my writhing cheeks as she worked her body against mine. All pain was forgotten as we rocked with wild abandon in a moist embrace; a timeless rhythm of Sapphic sensuality. Her finger sought the tight welcome of my anal blossom. I began to shudder as my orgasm rose, my growing ecstasy bringing Marijka to her own peak. We locked in mutual passion as our climax took hold. It overwhelmed us in a flooding surge, a crashing wave of ecstasy transporting us to the far shores of bliss. Our juices mingled in a sacred orgasmic communion.

We slept.

It was late when we were awakened next morning by the sound of our breakfast being laid in the suite's drawing room. In her typically organized fashion, Marijka had ordered us coffee, croissants and honey before retiring the previous night. There was a gentle knock on our bedroom door as the room-service maid entered and drew open the brocade curtains to allow the bright morning sunshine to flood the room. With a "Bonjour, Mesdames!" she tiptoed out again.

"The coffee can wait!" my conquisita murmured and leaned over me to suck at a rapidly hardening nipple through the gossamer film of my nightgown. I reached sleepily between her legs to finger the moist warmth of her pussy.

"Mmmmm!" she murmured and lay back, pulling up her lacy nightie to expose that ever-hungry cunt which I was soon to know so well.

16

"Your first duty each morning will be to suck me awake!"

So this was to be a more permanent arrangement? Not a one-night stand? My heart leapt with joy at the erotic vistas opening up before my eyes.

"Oh my darling Mistress!" I murmured ecstatically.

I put my head down between those Nordic limbs and began to fulfil my designated daily duty.

I pride myself on my cunnilingal ability! I sucked, nibbled and tongued my Mistress's exquisite pearl, coaxing it from its hooded concealment into hard and prominent arousal before darting my tongue and fingers into the musky recesses of her bower. I slurped her deliciously fragrant wetness greedily as it began to flow. She gripped my head savagely, pumping my face to her grinding conch, urging me to nuzzle even deeper into her soft furrowed recesses as she chased the smouldering glow that presaged the morning glory of her orgasmic release.

"Suck me, my sweet! You are my priestess! Worship at my Femina altar!" she panted hoarsely, wide-awake now and directing my ministrations. She wriggled and thrust her hips upward to meet my lips.

"Melt your 'Ice Queen'! Bring her to burning orgasm!"

My feverish tonguing worked in ardent frenzy and finally brought Mistress her explosive reward. She pressed my face fiercely against her pubes, rubbing my nose into her throbbing pearl, my forehead hard against the rippling muscles of her belly. She stiffened, clenched and unclenched her bottom cheeks clutched in my hands as her juices began to flow and then flood.

"Drink at my fountain! Drink from my grail!"

Marijka's legs shuddered as the orgasmic wave flowed through her. She clasped my head to the rictus of her cunt in joyful delirium. I lay still, bonded as one with Marijka, bathed in the sunrise of our morning passion.

The rest of the day was a jumbled blur of sensual highlights, joyful discovery and the growing realisation that my boss now regarded me as more than just a salaried slutslave at her beck and call.

We came again in a soapy lather of 'frigging lovesuds' in the shower amid golden taps and marble fittings. Later, we were driven to Grasse, Europe's centre of perfumery nestling in the hills above Nice, for a meeting with a master perfumier. It was here, as London's 'Ice Queen' discussed the creation of a range of Marijka Fragrances to be launched in Britain in time for the Christmas season, that I realised that my love for her was returned.

"Our first fragrance will be named 'Adele', after you," she said and gave me a French kiss.

I don't remember much about the day, after that! We lunched somewhere in Grasse and dined that night somewhere in Nice, but I don't remember where – I was too over the moon to notice such mundane things!

I remember the night, however! Marijka made love to me again in an explosion of passion that had our senses reeling. There was a full moon that night and she drew the drapes back to let a shaft of silvery light play on our lovebed.

She pulled back the covers. "Undress, my darling, and wait for your Mistress! I shall not keep you waiting long!"

Marijka appeared suddenly at the foot of the bed; a silent goddess-like statue bathed in silver. She stood there, a Viking 'Ice Queen'. She had strapped a rampant rod to her thighs; a rigidly erect long black dildo. It was an awesome sight in the pale moonlight. I lay awaiting my lover, my legs parted in welcome. I fingered my pussy provocatively, spreading wide the pink of my puffy labia to proffer my clitoral pearl to my conquisita.

"Come, my darling Mistress! Come and fill your special joyhole. Your English rose needs you. Her hot slutty slit craves your hard fuck."

I raised my pelvis and thrust a pillow under my tender butt. "Here it is, waiting for you to ride me. Bitch me! Bitch your slut! Did you enjoy spanking my pretty arse yesterday? Will you spank me again tomorrow? Come and fuck me, darling! Let me worship you with my body!. Smother my face with your warm, heavy titties!"

I started playing with my open pussy, rubbing my clit to hardness; enticing my 'Ice Queen' to melt in me.

She needed no encouragement. She slid between my legs without a word and thrust her black cock smoothly, deeply, powerfully, inch by inch into the enveloping tightness of my eager hole. I grunted, luxuriating in the fullness engendered by its rampant girth as I relaxed to accommodate the black beast of the night. Marijka pressed her lips to my gasping mouth, smothering my dirty talk, her tongue entwining with mine in a writhing serpentine frenzy. She began to pump her strong hips, impaling me on her weapon, thrusting the lance deep into the dark, slickness of my sluthole. Her thumping rhythm sent ripples of delight through my body from my hungry vagina. My cunt gripped my lover's magnificent weapon, massaging it with my juices as Marijka thrust and withdrew, thrust and withdrew…

"Oh my darling Mistress, fuck your Adele to heaven! I do love you so! Fuck your little English flower!"

My hips rose to meet Marijka's powerful thrusts. I took her gorgeous tits in my hands and squeezed them, kneaded them, pinched their hard nipples, clawed at those silvered pendulous roundels swaying before my eyes in the magic of moonlight. I urged her on to her desired orgasm, knowing she was taking me with her on her wild ride.

Marijka was riding me with hard, thumping frenzy now. I could feel her rising climax and knew that the alter-dildo in the grip of her vagina was rubbing her clit to bring her to that satisfying peak of ecstasy which I so desperately desired to give her.

"Fuck me, you dominating bitch! Ravish your English rose! Cock-whip your adoring Adele, you heavenly cunt-fucker! Rend me! Harder! Harder! You fucking bitch of a cockcunt!"

Marijka began to quiver, pant and gasp, coming in an explosive flash of orgasmic fire. She took my lips in passionate kisses, sucking, tonguing, biting, smothering. Nostrils flaring like a spent racehorse after the gallop, she clawed at my heaving back and bruised buttocks as she hammered home. The orgasm coursing through her body transmitted its energy to me, pinioned by her hammer, her juices seeping out around the leather harness to wet my belly and pussy. I joined her to come; quivering and shuddering in shared ecstasy. I locked my legs around my spent 'Queen', embracing her as our juices commingled in flooding orgasm.

Our B.A. Club Class flight back to London the following day, was doubly memorable. Marijka fired me as her Press Officer. That was the bad news. The good news came two minutes later accompanied by a glass of Champagne and a jeweller's presentation box in ice-blue velvet. It contained an enormous square-cut solitaire diamond ring.

Mistress Dominas and melted 'Ice Queens' don't ask – they command!

"Marry me!"

Ride A Horse – Ride A Cowboy
by Chloe Devlin

Cindy stood at the railing on the porch, watching the far corral where Jake was working with the horses. It was her third morning here on the ranch and she loved standing out here, drinking her coffee and watching Jake.

She'd come to Wyoming to escape the pressures of the city, but she hadn't expected to find herself attracted to one of the ranch hands on her uncle's ranch, especially Jake. But here she was getting up for the third early morning in a row. And she hated mornings.

Jake finished working with the sorrel and let her back into the main pen. He hopped over the fence and started for the main house. The boss's niece, Cindy, had been watching him for three straight mornings. He knew what she was looking at. And he knew what she wanted. Lucky for her that he wanted it too. But on his terms.

He'd been waiting for today 'cause he knew that no one else would be around for several hours. Plenty of time for his brand of fun and games with the filly. "You been watching me for a reason?"

"I like the way you handle the horses," she said.

"You want to be handled, too?"

She nodded, her eyes widening when he stepped up on the wooden porch. "Yeah, I think so."

"You gotta do more than 'think so'," he said. "Because I put my fillies through their paces. It's not easy, but it's

21

rewarding. I'll make you come more than you ever thought possible. I'll give you such pleasure you'll practically pass out. Think you can take it?"

He held his breath until she nodded again. Then he smiled, a wicked grin spreading across his tanned face. He explained the ground rules, telling her that he wouldn't harm her, but it might hurt at times. He then told her the safe word. "Use that word and I will drop everything and walk away for good. Is that understood?"

"Yes, sir."

He liked the way she called him sir. It showed she had the right frame of mind for the games to follow. "First thing, go back inside and take everything off. And I mean, everything. Then put on your highest pair of heels and come back out here."

There was only the slightest hesitation before she turned and walked back inside. As he waited for her to return, Jake mentally planned out what he would do. He knew that his gear was oiled and ready for use, even though it had been a while since he'd had such a beautiful filly to handle.

The floor creaked and he looked over at the doorway. Cindy stood there, wearing nothing but a pair of white heels, her body trim and fit. Her tits looked natural – no silicone grapefruits here – with luscious tight nipples that begged for his teeth. "Are these okay?" she asked. "I didn't bring much with me."

Jake felt his cock stiffen, pressing against the rough denim fabric of his jeans. "Just fine," he said quietly. "Just fine."

"Now what?"

He started to unbutton his shirt. "Now, you come over here and lay back on this table," he said. "Spread your legs wide. And then I'm gonna fuck you."

"Yes, sir." She shivered at his crude words, but she moved to obey his command.

Jake watched her intently as he continued to strip off his clothes. She moved well, gracefully. It looked like she worked out, too, her muscles toned and taut. If she fucked half as good as she looked, it was going to be a wonderful morning.

Cindy hoisted herself up on the rickety wooden table, feeling the rough wood scrape her buttocks. She couldn't believe she was actually going through with this. But Jake offered her an opportunity to experience something she'd always fantasized about. She felt herself moisten, knowing that, when she spread her legs, he would see how turned on she was.

It was a treat for her eyes as he pulled off his jeans, leaving him naked on the porch, his cock standing out from his flat belly. She wanted to run her hands over his abs, to feel them ripple in the sunlight. Then she leaned back until she was flat on the table. She had to roll her hips in order to spread her legs, so they draped over each side of the table.

She nearly jumped when she felt his hand on her inner thigh. Then his thick fingers began to stroke her, the calluses rubbing against her sensitive flesh. She shuddered as he circled her clit. Her entire crotch throbbed with desire and she knew it wouldn't take much to make her come. But would he?

A single finger sliding deep inside her pussy while another flicked her clit answered her question. Yes, he would. The sensations rapidly built up as she squirmed under his touch. Then another finger filled her and a third, stretching her muscles until she could feel the slight burn. He increased the fucking rhythm until he was quickly thrusting them in and out of her pussy.

Her muscles clamped down and she let out a shriek, the pleasure filling her body. "Oh! God, yes!"

With her body still convulsing in orgasm, he withdrew his fingers and swiftly shoved his cock into her. The added girth only made her come harder, panting for air. As she finally began to come down, she realized that he was still fucking her, his stiff dick thrusting in and out.

Jake reached down and grasped her thighs, lifting her legs so that her calves rested on his upper arms. Then with a grunt, he leaned forward and pistoned into her. A groan escaped his throat as he thrust one last time, leaving his cock buried in her as he filled her with his seed. The warm liquid squished out around his cock and dripped down the crack of her ass.

Still breathing heavily from his explosion, he slowly pulled out, her sheath clinging to his pole. "Okay. That was just to take the edge off. Now, we get into it."

Jake reached out and hauled Cindy to her feet. He noticed that her nipples were hard as berries, just begging for some attention. Bet they tasted just as sweet. Soon, he promised himself. But first things first.

Using some rope that had been left on the edge of the porch, he proceeded to tie her face-down over the edge of the porch, so that her tits hung free on one side and her legs barely reached the ground on the other. When she was completely secured, he stepped back, examining her from every side to make sure she was tied snugly.

He rested one hand on her ass, feeling her tense. The skin was cool and smooth to his touch. But it wouldn't remain that way for very long. He intended to warm her butt very nicely. "How many?" he asked.

"How many what?"

"Swats. How many times should I spank you?"

"I don't know. Whatever … pleases you, sir."

He smiled. "Good answer. I think fifteen on each cheek will do to start."

Without further comment, he began spanking her upturned buttocks. It wasn't hard to fall into a steady rhythm, whacking away. After a few minutes, her cheeks began to turn red and the heat in her skin warmed his palm. He enjoyed the tingle that spread through his arm every time he made contact.

Each time he hit her, she grunted, but otherwise, she remained silent as he finished the spanking. It wasn't meant to be a punishment spanking, just a prelude to the rest of the fun. By the time he finished, his hand was beginning to ache and he knew that her butt hurt. It had to. He'd turned the delicate skin a bright red, no splotches or bruises, just tenderized. Perfect for the next phase of his game.

He stepped off the porch so he could face her. "Are you

ready to learn how to ride?"

She looked up at him, her face nearly as red as her ass. "But I know how to ride."

"Not the way I teach it," he replied. "My method is very special. Now wait here while I get your horse saddled."

Cindy kept her head lifted as she watched Jake head for the barn, wearing only his boots. She wished she could use her hands to rub her butt. It stung like wildfire. But she couldn't deny the pleasure his spanking had produced either. She had almost come while he was hitting her. She'd had to bite her lip to keep from crying out with pleasure, feeling the moisture from her arousal trickle down her inner thighs.

Jake brought out Sky, the gelding she'd been riding. But instead of her usual saddle, he had on one she didn't recognize. She blinked to make sure she was seeing clearly. It looked like there was more than one protrusion on the saddle. More than the pommel horn.

After tying the horse to the railing, he came back and began to untie her from her perch on the porch, explaining as he worked. "That's a special saddle I had custom-made," he said. "It has a locking mechanism in the middle of the seat. I can attach one of several implements there. I promised you plenty of orgasms. And this will provide the first set of 'em."

As he stood her upright, she felt her spine stretch and crack in relief. Jake led her down the steps until she was next to the horse. "Notice that there are two dildos attached. I plan to plug both your holes for this training session. Now, step up here so I can get you situated."

Gingerly, she stepped onto a large mounting block with Jake, following his instructions to swing her leg over, but not sit down until he had lined up the twin dildos. It had been so long since she'd experienced double penetration. Not since that night in –

She let out a groan as both shafts filled her pussy and asshole. When she had seated herself completely, she clenched her inner muscles experimentally, discovering the delight squeezing the toys could bring her.

Jake strapped her legs to the side of the horse, the leather supple against her skin, not giving her the stirrups for support. Then her hands were tied together and then to the pommel horn. Feelings of complete submission flooded her. How had he known? When she hadn't ever realized that she craved a strong man in the bedroom.

"Now, we'll go through all the training paces." Jake untied the horse, leading its bound rider into the main corral.

Cindy could scarcely believe the sensations that soared through her body. It was as though she was instantaneously on the edge of an orgasm. 0-60 in nothing flat. She gasped with each step the horse took. Each time a hoof set down, pleasure jarred through her body. She wouldn't be able to last long like this. She was too turned on.

Jake let out the lead on the training rope so that he could snap his whip and send the gelding in a circle around him. The sun beat down on her naked body and sweat began to bead and trickle its way down between her breasts. Underneath her spread thighs, the leather gently rubbed against her hot flesh.

At first, he was content to let the horse simply walk around. But after a couple of revolutions, he flicked his wrist. The whip snapped and the gelding began to trot.

Without the support of stirrups, the bumpy gait of the gelding slammed the twin dildos in and out of both her holes. Her muscles tightened as an orgasm ripped through her body. She threw back her head and screamed. "Oh, God! Jake! Oh, my God!"

Just as the first waves of pleasure began to subside, the gelding's gait changed. The bumps smoothed out into a gentle canter. But the rocking chair action ratcheted her pleasure higher. Another set of waves buffeted her body. As she arched her back, her nipples ached, and she wished she – or Jake – could hold and pinch them. She stiffened, then slumped over the horse's neck. With her hands tied to the pommel, she could hardly keep herself from sliding to one side or the other, but the straps at her ankles kept her from sliding completely off the horse.

She gasped, her pussy twitching as yet another orgasm flashed through her. "Ohgodohgodohgod," she panted, the lack of oxygen making her vision go fuzzy for a moment.

"Whoa, boy," Jake said, slowing the gelding to a slow walk. "Sit up, Cindy," he ordered. "No slouching on the job."

Jake watched as Cindy slowly straightened her back until she was upright and off the horse's neck. One part of him wanted to make sure she was okay, but he knew she had to be. Otherwise, she would've said the safe word. But all she'd done was cry out to him and God.

He was still rock hard and aching. Fucking Cindy hadn't even taken the edge off his need. He couldn't wait any longer for their ride together.

"Ready, Cindy?" he called out.

She stared back at him with lust in her eyes, panting so hard she couldn't speak. He brought Sky back to the mounting block. Leaving her hands bound together, he released them from the saddle and undid the straps on her thighs. "Raise up," he commanded. "Just enough to release the dildos."

As soon as she was free, he swiftly removed the drenched double-dildo and replaced it with a single shaft that was wider and longer. "You're so wet, I practically don't need any lube. But we wouldn't want to hurt you, so …"

He slathered some oil on the massive fake dick, then on his own aching shaft. Fisting his cock, he made sure that every inch was coated in the warm lube.

As he stepped up on the mounting block, he said, "After I climb into the saddle, I want you to sit back down. This time I'm going to be the cock in your ass."

A shudder ran through her body, but when he tilted her head around, he saw nothing but longing in her gaze. Unable to resist the temptation of her tongue poking out of her mouth, he swiftly covered her lips with his, letting his tongue sweep through her sweetness, tasting her desire.

When he lifted his head, they were both panting for breath. "Do you understand?" he managed to say.

"Yes, sir."

His dick stiffened even more, if that was possible. Sure that his balls were going to explode, he climbed into the leather saddle that was wet with her juices.

As she sank back down, he guided his cock straight up into her tight ass. He sucked in a breath at the heat that enveloped his dick, the muscles that gripped him. "Damn. You have one of the hottest, tightest asses I've ever been in."

Experimentally he tightened his muscles, feeling himself sink deeper into her.

She whimpered and flung her head back against his shoulder. "Oh, Jake. So big. Feels so good."

"You're going to feel even better, baby," he promised, bringing his arms around her.

With one hand, he grasped the reins and guided the horse away from the hitching post. With his other, he grasped one breast, squeezing and massaging until his fingers gripped only the taut nipple. The tighter he gripped, the more she clenched her muscles around his cock. Not wanting her to explode too soon, he released the nipple and cupped the entire mound.

"No one's at the far south pasture," he murmured in her ear. "Ready for a nice long ride?"

She gave a laugh. "I think so."

"Okay. Here we go." Clucking to the gelding, he increased the horse's gait to a fast walk.

Cindy felt the rhythm of the horse change slightly beneath her thighs, the quickening percussion of hoof beats vibrating up through the dildo in her pussy and Jake's cock in her ass.

She'd come so many times already she'd lost count. Now it was just one long continuous sensation washing through her body. She'd never known that feelings like this existed, an exquisite sensation that was so pleasurable it was almost painful.

Flinging her arms up and back around his neck, she held on tightly. The action thrust out her chest, her ripe nipples begging for attention again. She shivered as he flicked them repeatedly.

"Time to go faster," Jake said.

Before she could reply, she felt his thighs tighten against hers, the pressure spurring the gelding into a canter, then immediately into a gallop. The wind whistled past her face, whipping the short blonde strands of her hair around. She shook them free of her eyes and stared straight ahead as the landscape flew past.

Jake kept one arm banded around her waist so he could maintain the steady rhythm of his thrusts. Combined with the pounding of the dildo in her pussy, Cindy knew she was being pushed to the very edge of her limits. But she didn't want any of it to stop. The wind, the horse, the dildo, Jake's cock – it was the most unbelievable experience of her life.

The horse's gait changed slightly, slowing from a mad gallop into the smooth rocking of a gentle canter. Cindy caught her breath, the sweet smell of cut grass filtering through the warmth of the sun and mingling with the animal scent of the horse.

She turned her head so her lips were inches from Jake's mouth. "I could do this forever," she said. "You feel so good inside me."

"Ready for one more hard gallop, baby?"

She kissed him hard, then nodded. "Oh, yes! Let's go!"

Once again, the big animal beneath them responded, his powerful muscles bunching as he ran flat out. The sensations crowded in, flooding over Cindy until she thought she'd go crazy from the sheer intensity.

Relaxing her inside muscles as much as she could, she savored every thrust of Jake's cock gliding up her ass in counterpoint to the sweet movement of the dildo in her cunt. Shudders shook her body, buffeting her as she writhed in ecstasy.

"God! Jake! Yes, that's it! I'm coming!" she screamed at the top of her lungs.

Tears streamed from her eyes, blinding her to the images around her, forcing her to focus on the sensations thundering through her body. She stiffened, every muscle locked in the wildest pleasure imaginable. Then, she heard Jake give a hoarse shout, then felt the warmth of his seed he reached his own riveting climax, coming deep inside her ass.

Slumping back against his sweat-slick body, she gasped for breath, wondering if her heart was going to pound right out of her chest. Jake's heart thumped against her back, his heavy breathing rasping in her ear. The pounding lessened as the horse slowed its gait – from heart-stopping gallop to smooth canter and finally into a rocking-chair walk.

"Here it is," he said, still breathless. "The far south pasture. Want to take a short break before we ride back?"

Cindy took several deep breaths, tingles still running through her. "Oh yeah. I think you've given new meaning to that country-western song."

"Which one?"

"'Save A Horse (Ride A Cowboy)'."

"Ah, that one."

"Yeah, we should rename it. 'Ride A Horse – Ride A Cowboy'!"

Jake's laughter echoed over the empty pasture. "Anytime, baby. We can go riding anytime you want."

Girls Who Wear Glasses?
by Laurel Aspen

Tara blinked, opened her eyes and then instantly closed them. Oh God the light was so bright, searing her befuddled, barely functioning brain. What time was it? Oh no 11am, she never usually slept this late, half the day gone. Which day? Tara struggled to recall and opened her eyes again, just a fraction, enough to squint myopically at the digital clock next to her bed. Sunday. Yes, that was right, Sunday, because on Saturday evening she'd been at party. From which she'd somehow returned, thankfully to her own bed. Gingerly she began an appraisal of her body, checking for damage and clues as to what had gone on the previous night. OK, start at the top. Christ her head hurt; headache, parched mouth, sore throat, slight metallic taste; too much red wine you stupid cow. Skin dry, last night's makeup clogging her pores, limbs aching from the effects of unconsciousness replacing proper sleep.

Tara hesitantly lifted the duvet. A skimpy silk vest, part of her party outfit remained mercifully in place but no sign of her bra. Knickers - or more correctly an equally skimpy thong also in situ - so it appeared she hadn't scored. Thank goodness, if she'd been as pissed as her complaining body seemed to be indicating heaven knows what might have happened. At which tenuously comforting thought the bedroom door opened and an all too cheerful voice brightly announced: 'Morning. Breakfast, if you can bear the idea, is served. Fresh coffee, toast and marmalade.' Yeah, it smelt good and Tara was suddenly aware of feeling both hungry and thirsty, but who the hell was her benefactor? She fumbled for her glasses, eventually locating them under her pillow. Good job she hadn't worn her contacts last night and crashed out in them or she wouldn't be able to see at all. Perching the round wire frames on the end of her retrouse nose she peered inquiringly at the tall, nice looking, pretty much fully dressed and vaguely familiar male in front of her.

'Ah yes,' he smiled, 'your expression speaks volumes.'

I'm guessing something along the lines of: '"Oh God, what time is it? What did I do last night? Who the hell is that?"'

Tara forced a wan smile, whoever he was the empathic stranger at least appeared house trained and unthreatening.

'That's pretty much about it,' she confessed sheepishly.

'Jack, Jack Selby,' he introduced himself to her for the second time in 12 hours, 'we met at my cousin's do last night. You were apparently celebrating something.'

He raised a quizzical eyebrow.

'Yes,' she replied briefly, sipping the coffee gratefully but declining to elaborate. Tara didn't usually take sugar but black and sweet was just the job to kick-start her into full consciousness. 'Penny's do,' she continued, 'weren't we talking at some point?'

'For much of the latter part of the evening, I'm delighted confirm,' smiled Jack, 'got on rather well I thought, you invited me back here at any rate.'

'Did I? Tara was puzzled. 'Sorry,' she added quickly, 'no offence, but I wouldn't normally do that on a first meeting.'

'No, fair enough,' responded Jack easily. 'In my defence I'd cite the fact that Penny introduced us and there did seem to be quite a strong mutual attraction.'

'We were snogging in the taxi weren't we?' asked Tara rhetorically, as another fragment of not at all unpleasant recall flashed through her jumbled synapses.

'And here too,' agreed Jack, 'after which, well things went a bit awry.'

'Oh Christ what did I do?'

'Do you really want to know?'

'No, but sooner or later it's going to come back to haunt me, best get it over with.'

'OK,' leaning on the doorframe Jack regaled Tara with an edited version of events while she enthusiastically consumed her unexpected breakfast in bed.

'After some pretty hot and heavy kissing and groping you decided we needed more wine.'

Wordlessly Tara buried her head in her hands.

'It's alright,' he added quickly, 'I managed to dissuade you,'

'Thank you,' she said quietly.

'It then transpired that in addition to an absolutely wonderful pair of legs you have extremely sensitive nipples.'

Tara blushed. 'Which would explain the absence of my bra this morning no doubt. What exactly was I wearing?'

'When we first met the same top and thong as now, plus skin-tight faded jeans - showcased your fantastic bum to perfection as no doubt you intended - and perilously high heeled sandals on which you swayed ever more dangerously as the night wore on.'

'Don't worry,' Jack added as an after thought, 'you didn't start jettisoning clothes until we got back here.'

'I played Steely Dan's "Reeling in the Years" on the stereo didn't I?' sighed Tara.

'Yeah, what made you remember that?'

'I don't, I just have a tendency to follow the same pattern when pissed; loud rock music accompanied by an impromptu striptease. What happened after that?'

'Um, you became rather aroused,' explained Jack, 'and suggested that - not to put too fine a point on it ...'

'I'd benefit from a good stiff cock?' Tara completed the sentence, flushing scarlet. 'Oh Jack I'm so sorry.'

'Hey no need to be, it was the best suggestion I'd heard in months. Trouble was the alcohol had clearly hit you hard so it just wasn't on. You really didn't know what was happening and there was no way I could take advantage.'

Tara's face lost its smile, this was no longer amusing, she'd put herself in real danger.

'I mean I wanted to but…' Jack let the sentence trail away.

'Anyhow,' he continued brightly, 'so's not to hurt your feelings I claimed not to have any condoms.'

'Did it work?'

'No, you said "sod it let's do it anyway."'

'Oh shit!'

'I managed to talk you out of that too, only to for you to go of on another tack and decide I deserved a blow job.'

Tara's blush turned beetroot. 'I always find it helps break the ice with strangers,' she said with heavy irony.

Jack grinned again, a boyish sparkle in his eyes, 'anyway you dived at me, unzipped my jeans, pressed your face to my crotch, and promptly fell asleep. Obviously I was flattered; I guess it must be my charisma.'

'Jack, I'm so sorry, I don't know what to say.'

'How about "I'll meet you for tea this afternoon?" When you've had a chance to recover, at the café in the park across the road.'

'You want to see me again?' Tara couldn't believe it.

'Of course,' said Jack simply.

'But I behaved so badly…'

'True, but come on, everyone's done something similar, I mean it's not as if you make a habit of it.'

'I really don't, honestly,' said Tara fervently, 'I haven't done anything that stupid since I was student. But why, after such a performance would you want to risk another encounter.'

'Because you're smart, funny and good looking for starters.' Tara began to object but Jack silenced her with a gently raised hand. 'Honest, self-deprecating and not up your own arse like so many writers.'

'How do you know I'm a writer?'

'Meet me at the café and find out. Look I must dash, places to be, folks to see. Four o'clock alright?'

'Thank you kind and chivalrous sir, I accept.'

Jack was already there when Tara turned up. His back was toward her and she took a moment to privately assess his physical appearance. Slender and sunburned, the sleeves of his worn but expensive linen shirt turned back to reveal muscular forearms and the tantalising hint of a tattoo. As if he sensed her presence, Jack turned and smiled.

'Hi Tara, feeling better?'

'Much thanks, perhaps, 'cos I rarely have them my hangovers are thankfully short-lived, plenty of mineral water and a long shower does wonders for a girl.'

'I see you've dressed to impress again.'

Tara took the compliment with good grace. Why not? She'd spent the last hour making sure she looked great. A floaty, almost see-through top, short flared skirt, black sheer tights and knee-length, narrow-heeled boots.

'When you're short of bosom it's best to divert attention to other assets, in my case the long legs you mentioned,' she said, sitting elegantly down.

'Don't be so self-critical, I have fond - albeit brief - memories of your boobs,' grinned Jack wickedly.

'Oh good another conversation which begins with me blushing.'

After which opening pleasantries she did her damdest to find out more about Jack. Without a deal of success for his replies were pleasantly opaque and the conversation invariably skilfully diverted back to her. Jack, she gathered, travelled, took pictures on commission for galleries and publishers and, well that was pretty much it. A good listener, he obviously preferred talking about others, except to flavour the discourse with the odd tantalising anecdote.

'So you're a writer,' he said at length

'How did you know?' replied Tara, recalling the earlier revelation.

'Because Penny said you were a freelance journo and because the reason for your secret celebration is on your kitchen table.'

A cold hand clutched at her stomach, Tara's face went pale, and she suddenly felt as if the life had drained from her soul.

'You found...'

'Tara I wasn't searching, but the book and the letter were there when I made the coffee. Sure I admit it, in the hour or so while I waited for you to surface I read some of your short stories, but then they are now in the public domain. Although under a *nom de plume*; "Ms Celia Strictland".

'Not fair, that was the publisher's suggestion, this is the first book I've done, I didn't like to argue,' mumbled Tara, gaze downcast.

Jack continued, ebulliently.

'Amazing stuff, erotic fiction for women with a CP theme. Your writing is extremely talented, page-turning narrative, good characterisation and very, um, stimulating action. You've one hell of an imagination Tara, unless your fiction is based upon experience?'

Tara knew a loaded question when asked. 'It's all hypothetical,' she ventured after a lengthy pause.

'Something must have informed this interest,' he pressed.

'Ever since I hit puberty spanking is something I've imagined,' Tara ventured cautiously.

'So always in sexual context?' Jack was clearly intrigued.

'Absolutely,' confirmed Tara, 'I had liberal parents who'd be appalled at the idea of hitting a child and corporal punishment was rightly abolished in schools years before I began my education. For ages I've dreamt of being spanked, become aroused by my own feverish imaginings. Heck, since this turning into a spontaneous confessional I've frequently masturbated to punishment fantasies.' Tara's eyes blazed fervently. 'It's probably hard to credit but you're the first person I've ever admitted this to.'

'And in these romanticised daydreams you're always taken to task by a male?'

'I know, dreadful isn't it? A feminist's worst nightmare,' Tara giggled beguilingly as she sipped her coffee, 'yes, emancipated as I am in real life, I always envisage being

36

mastered by a muscly bloke.'

'But if you've never experienced a spanking how do you know enough to write stories about it?

'Well the stories aren't solely about spanking,' pouted Tara, not best pleased by this slight on her credibility. 'There's a lot of sex included and that's something of which I do have pretty broad and direct knowledge. Besides, I've sneaked into town and bought magazines, books similar to the one I've recently written. Even purchased a few expensive and mostly disappointing DVDs.'

'Disappointing?'

'The British ones are obsessed with the punitive aspect and it's always some horrid ugly old bloke beating a beautiful young woman. As if! I have seen an excellent US DVD with a plausible plot line, an attractive couple and a spanking which really turned the girl on, culminating in believable sex.'

'Closer to your ideal?' Jack leaned forward; the conversation was becoming progressively more intimate.

'Yeah, similar to my stories. Not surprisingly since I started writing them for personal amusement. I began after reading some of the stuff in the shops and realised I could do better.'

Tara stopped, aware she'd monopolised the conversation for most of the last 10 minutes. Once again Jack had contrived to get her talking about herself.

'Enough imagining,' he said decisively, 'time to experience a real-life spanking I suggest.'

She hadn't seen this coming. 'What!' Tara was genuinely shocked. 'You mean you and me?'

'You know you can trust me, last night demonstrated that.'

'True enough and I'm grateful really but...' Tara's brain was a whirl, the idea was by no means immediately abhorrent, quite the reverse in fact, there was certainly something commanding about Jack and physically he was definitely her type of guy. And wasn't this exactly the sort of scenario she'd invented a 100 times?

'Last night also showed you acting in a foolhardy, very

risky way. Hardly responsible adult behaviour and eminently worthy of punishment,' Jack wasn't going to let Tara off the hook.

'How come you're so expert?' she replied, a hint of desperation in her tone.

'Not expert but my life has fortunately proved varied,' said Jack easily.

'And you've spanked women before?'

'Oh yes,' said Jack with a smile which managed to remain just the right side of smug, characteristically he didn't elaborate. 'So Tara,' he went on in an assured tone. 'Let's assume the principal of your punishment is agreed so there remains only the detail to be thrashed – sorry, couldn't resist it – out, what's an appropriate penalty for such delinquent behaviour do you suppose?'

'I get spanked,' began Tara tentatively, hardly able to believe she was speaking the words. 'Over your knee,' she added hesitantly, 'on my bottom,' her voice sunk to almost a whisper, 'skirt up and knickers down probably,' she could no longer look Jack in the face, 'on my bare bottom. Quite hard.'

'Goes without saying,' replied Jack nonchalantly, 'these are serious misdemeanours young lady. And what else what might you have in your flat which could be pressed into service?'

'I, I...' Overcome with nerves, Tara couldn't find her voice.

Her face burned, a shiver of anticipation coursed through her veins, a sharp twinge of arousal simultaneously assailed her groin.

'Speak up please,' Jack demanded firmly.

'About a year ago I bought a leather paddle in one of those new women-only sex shops. I loved the feel, so tactile, and the smell, so evocative.' Tara clenched her fists tightly forcing the words out in a rush. 'I tried using it; sort of self-flagellation but that didn't really work. I'm sure you could apply it expertly.'

Well that was it, in the words of the old soul classic: "Signed, sealed, delivered I'm yours baby."

'Yes I'm sure you're right,' responded Jack calmly, leaving enough cash on the table to cover their drinks and taking Tara by the hand. Back at her flat Jack moved purposefully and with a minimum of conversation. Seating himself in an upright chair he beckoned Tara to him. 'I shall begin by administering a sound spanking' he announced shortly, 'it is entirely in your interest to cooperate, to which end start by raising your skirt clear of your behind and get across my knee.' Heart pounding, knees knocking, Tara obeyed, slowly gathering the hem of the diminutive garment and hesitantly gathering it around her waist. Rather than the expected expression of approval Jack glared at her.

'I don't like tights,' he said shortly, 'in future stockings and suspenders or bare legs under a skirt please Tara.'

'Future?' thought Tara momentarily but had no time to pursue the notion being suddenly more preoccupied with her new undignified position facing the carpet. Head down, toes on the floor she waited apprehensively not daring to look over her shoulder.

'Hang on a minute,' said Jack irritably after a moment's pause, 'stand up again please.'

Puzzled by this untoward turn of events Tara struggled to her feet.

'I know from previous experience just how hard these wretched garments are to remove once you're in position,' grunted Jack crossly, 'consequently we'll have them down now.' So saying he tugged her tights and knickers into a tangle around her knees.

Tara gasped in shock and surprise.

'It's no good complaining girl,' continued Jack firmly, 'you've only yourself to blame and as a consequence of presenting yourself inappropriately attired we'll start on the bare.'

'But you never specified what clothes I was expected to wear,' wailed Tara indignantly.

'Of course not,' responded Jack crisply, 'why should I? Tell me Tara, how many of your CP stories feature what our US cousins inelegantly term pantyhose?'

'Fair point,' conceded Tara and prudently ceased complaining while being upended for the second time in as many minutes. Once more she waited, tensing her buttock cheeks against the anticipated first blow.

'We can linger like this all day,' announced Jack calmly, 'although I suspect you'll fairly quickly find this arrangement uncomfortable. Or,' he continued sarcastically, 'you can relax your buttocks and allow me to begin'.

Easier said than done but somehow an increasingly nervous Tara complied.

'Better,' grunted Jack grudgingly and commenced spanking; lightly at first his palm skimming the surface to visit the merest suggestion of a stinging impact to Tara's porcelain globes. It was, she initially considered, endurable. Indeed the resultant mild smarting sensation coupled with the realisation that here she was, at last, surrendered, bare-bottomed and helpless across a demonstrably handsome man's knee. It proved a considerable turn on.

As the minutes ticked by, Jack gradually increased the pace and power of each spank, cupping his hand slightly to increase the sound of each percussive impact. Tara enjoyed the ripples each subsequent slap sent shuddering through her taut flesh. Ah, it was beginning to smart now, Tara's feet kicked out involuntarily and she gasped and wiggled across his lap as the heat in her bottom began to inexorably increase. Her bottom felt as if were positively glowing, 'Oh no,' she groaned, squirming on his lap, 'enough already, it's starting to hurt.'

'The purpose of spanking being what exactly?' observed Jack wryly. 'If it ain't hurting it ain't working,' he added as, satisfied with the warmth radiating from her scarlet-hued upper cheeks, he switched his attentions to Tara's lower posterior curves.

'Ow no!'

Tara's indignant gyrations became ever more animated

and, despite the constraint of her tangled hosiery, she unintentionally parted her legs far wider than was prudent to maintain any vestige of modesty.

Jack smiled; she'd obviously been entirely truthful when hinting at being no novice with regard to matters sexual. Tara's pudenda were completely clean-shaven, her labial lips clearly exposed and glistening with the unmistakeable evidence of incipient arousal. He paused from spanking her delectable rear to savour the sight then, carefully taking each labium between finger and thumb, rubbed them delicately together. Tara groaned ecstatically in response and continued to do so with loud abandon for the next few minutes as her moist secrets were expertly petted and probed. An assured thumb circled her clitoris and stroked her own juices around her puckered anus. Deft fingers slipped into her hot, wet vagina and began to delve deeper and faster into her honeyed portal. Moans of pleasure escaped her as she writhed across his lap, trapped between pleasure and pain, her arousal increasing by the moment. Tara raised her arse without inhibition, inviting the resumption of contact with his punishing palm, while at the same moment pushing back her pubis; the better to enjoy his urgent finger-fucking of her hungry sex. Her climax came quickly and violently, arching her body in intense physical pleasure as Tara was smacked and penetrated to a noisy release.

'Did that meet your expectations?' enquired Jack finally as she lay dishevelled, satiated and breathing heavily across his knee.

'More intense than I ever imagined,' confirmed Tara fervently.

'Remember, you still have a dose of the paddle to come and I don't think you'll find that so user-friendly,' said Jack. 'Go and fetch it please.'

Her maiden spanking had clearly had a salutary effect as, knickers and tights still half way down her thighs and bottom glowing red Tara obediently hobbled to the bedroom to fetch the instrument of correction.

'How do you want me?' she enquired meekly upon her return.

Jack allowed the moment of hushed expectancy to last the better part of a minute while he examined the shiny leather implement she handed him.

'Beautifully made,' he murmured, 'finest quality material, look at the grain. Excellent,' he soliloquised, turning the paddle over and slapping it experimentally against his palm.

Tara winced as a sound like a pistol shot echoed around the room.

'Hand-tooled, beautiful stitching,' Jack continued his eulogy, 'and specifically designed for just one purpose,' he fixed her with a steely look, 'to make the bare bottoms of irresponsible young women extremely hot and sore.'

Tara winced again, hands clutching at her still hot moons. Her look mutely beseeched mercy.

'How do I want you?' said Jack returning to her question, 'with as few encumbrances as possible. Take off those damn tights, knickers, skirt; the lot in fact. Then put the killer boots back on, their high heels will tense your calves and push that pert little arse out nicely. Oh, and keep the glasses on too. Not only do I find them irrepressibly cute but I want you to witness your hiding."

Heart thumping, thighs trembling, Tara hurried to obey. A cool breeze from the window brushed across her fair skin as she obediently stripped of her outfit. Small boobs aside she was proud of her gamine frame and endless legs. The spanking hadn't been so bad, the thrill of masculine contact – strong hands bending her to his will, everything she hoped for in endless girlish imaginings – had made her come uninhibitedly after all. That said though, somehow the prospect of a leathering with the paddle was good deal scarier, guaranteed to hurt her already sore behind. Now that it came to the crunch, what if she wasn't brave at all, just how cruel would Jack be? Yet perversely these very doubts, the fear of the unknown, proved to possess aphrodisiacal qualities. Pulling on the boots she stood up straight, thrust her breasts and shaven pubis thrust proudly forward and, every nerve ending tingling with anticipation, faced her tormentor.

Christ but she looked gorgeous, thought Jack who was finding it increasingly difficult to resist the temptation to sweep Tara from her feet, carry her straight to the sofa and bend her to his wicked way. Instead he cupped each of her outthrust little tits in his hands, felt her shiver with pleasure as he softly squeezed them taking each erect nipple between finger and thumb and gently twisting.

'Oooooh,' a low moan escaped Tara's lips, the sensation was exquisite. Her knees felt weak and Tara's tongue circled her lips in lascivious pleasure, inviting his kiss.

'You little trollop, you're really turned on aren't you,' announced Jack fondly running his hands appreciatively down the front of her naked body, across her flat hard abdomen to the junction of her thighs.

'Look at you, sopping wet again,' he said holding a glistening finger before her bespectacled eyes as evidence of her body's betrayal. 'Far too much pleasure for a girl destined to be punished, time to turn around, bend over and touch your toes.'

Tara needed no second bidding and being enviably young, supple and fit easily achieved the required stance. Bent almost double, legs apart, perfect peach of a bottom pushed out for his delectation, her denuded sex glistened lewdly.

Not trusting himself to observe any longer Jack stood back, raised his arm and delivered the first blow

CRACK!

'Oooh yaaa!' Tara yelled out in pain and surprise as her left buttock absorbed the brunt of the unexpectedly severe impact. 'Christ that hurt,' she gasped, grimacing at the pain

WHACK!

'Yeeow, shit!' she cried in outrage as an identical blow struck the right cheek. Both buttocks now stung fiercely, their entire surface throbbing with what seemed to Tara an unendurable hurt.

WHACK!

43

'Aaaah!' Hands loosing their grip on her ankles and flailing before her, Tara half rose from her jacknifed pose.

'Get back down girl,' growled Jack unsympathetically and in the knick of time she managed to resume her position. Only half way there. 'Oh Christ,' Tara moaned, 'that smarts.' The burning flesh of her poor bum felt as if it had been stretched drum-tight then flayed.

WOP!

'Ooof, Omigod! That was too low!' With a wail of anguish Tara gyrated frantically her damaged derriere, providing Jack with an undignified display of her bottom crack. Oh this was torture, far worst than she'd ever anticipated. Craning her neck she peered over her shoulder to discover her already pink bottom was now further decorated with livid marks, which looked as if they might take days to fade.

SLAP!

'Yeow!' Unable to control her reaction Tara shot uptight, the pure burning pain bringing tears to her eyes. Her hands clutched her blazing bum. Jack however was in no mood for clemency. Tara's first time must be hard; be firm now, he'd decided and ensure total obedience in the future. Within minutes the fiery sting would mutate into a warm, insidiously spreading sensual glow, but as yet Tara remained a novice still to discover such compensations. With a firm hand in the centre of her back he forced the snivelling girl back down and delivered the last stroke.

CRACK!

'Oh Oh Oh!' Tara was immediately upright again and performing an anguished jig in front of him.

'Oh hellfire Jack, thank fuck that's it, I couldn't take any more,' she wailed in obviously genuine distress.

'Oh but you will young lady.'

'What? You've already given me six.'

'Six of the best may work for the purposes of your fictional encounters, Tara, but someone who's behaved as badly as you gets a full dozen in real life. Risking unsafe sex with stranger when drunk deserves a proper hiding.'

'Oh but my poor little bottom, it's agony, I can't possibly stay in that position,' Tara cried.

'No, you're right in that respect,' conceded Jack. 'I think bending over will have to be abandoned for the moment. In fact since you seem to find it impossible to stay down I may have to employ the diaper position.

'What's that when it's at home?' enquired Tara suspiciously.

'On your back, knees up to your chest, ankles in the air; that way I can hold your legs and beat your bum,' responded Jack casually.

'No way, too degrading, besides you might accidentally hit my pussy,' pleaded Tara.

'So what do you suggest? Because believe me Tara, that arse yours is going to be properly punished,' declared Jack.

'Alright, alright, let me kneel with something to hold onto, I can do this Jack, please don't humiliate me,' replied Tara plaintively.

'Hmm, good idea. Let's have you on that chair in front of the mirror. That's it kneel up, hold onto the back and push that bottom right out for me. Good, now what can you see?'

'An unforgiving brute about to make my poor stinging bottom hurt even more than it already does,' moaned Tara petulantly, nevertheless proffering her perfect peaches just as Jack directed.

'Correct,' agreed Jack unabashed, 'now then my beautiful bespectacled miscreant, watch closely.' So saying he bought the paddle ringing down across her rear. Despite her animated wriggling and yelps of complaint Tara's concluding chastisement was applied far less severely.

WHACK! WHACK! WHACK!

Three slaps fell in quick succession upon her lower curves, just above the tender junction of buttock and thigh.

'OOOOH!' she shrieked, frantically kicking her booted feet but managing to stay in place.

CRACK! CRACK! CRACK! The final trio were resolutely delivered to the tops of her thighs

'URGH, Jack!' For the first time she'd called his name and in a tone – if Jack wasn't mistaken – tinged with an implicit acceptance of her to submission to him. As the cumulative smart seared her hindquarters, Tara shook her head vigorously and almost dislodged her glasses.

'Is that it, can I rub?' she enquired ruefully, one hand already sneaking towards her ravaged rear while the other pushed her specs back onto the bridge of her nose.

'Yes you may,' confirmed Jack, 'but I'm not quite through.'

'And does the "not quite" have anything to do with the lethal looking bulge in your trousers?' asked Tara archly.

'Correct,' agreed Jack grasping her hips purposefully.

'And I suppose you think I'm going to let you put that monster inside me?' Tara was rapidly regaining her composure. 'Oh!' she added quickly as Jack did so.

With a triumphal grin Tara ground her hot buttocks back into his firm abdomen, urging him on. Beginning with long, slow, steady strokes that soon rapidly increased in tempo, Jack felt her inner muscles grip his rampant cock, sending jolts of sublime pleasure coursing through his fevered loins. Tara arched her back, cried out and came a second time. Pausing only to withdraw his cock James reached orgasm, spurting jolts of thick, hot semen across her tenderised buttocks then rubbing it into the velvet skin.

A short time later their respective roles, while not reversed, certainly seemed to be in transition. Announcing firmly 'I've not yet finished with you my lad,' Tara bade Jack sit on the chair whereupon she sank to her knees and began to skilfully revive his flagging manhood with her mouth and tongue. With her glasses perched incongruously upon her nose Jack thought Tara resembled a pretty but preoccupied academic. Had he included the soubriquet "Professor" this would in fact have been a completely correct assessment.

'You know that old saying, that men don't make passes...' he began.

'At girls who wear glasses? Load of old rubbish,' averred Tara decisively. 'Anyway, how about girls who wear glasses making passes in order to get spanked arses?'

The Good Girl
by Emily Dubberley

I don't know what made me do it: I've always been a good
girl. As a kid, I worked hard at school, went to bed when I was
told to and didn't think about shoplifting, sneaking out to
parties or even wearing make up (other than the clear lip-gloss
and brown mascara allowed by my mum). University was
about getting my degree. OK, there were a few drunken nights
– I'm not the dullest person on the planet – but I attended all
my lectures, even the 9 a.m. ones, and never let a party night
interfere with my essay deadlines. I was in my first job within
a week of graduation and, since then, I've been steadily
working my way up the career ladder. Now, aged 30, I'm
Marketing Director for a global brand that you'd know if I
named it, with a beautiful two-bed flat in an up-and-coming
part of town and a life that, to any outside observer, looks
flawless.

Most of the time I'd be inclined to agree. I can afford to buy
designer clothes, stock my fridge with Waitrose's finest and
go on exotic holidays. Although my job's stressful, my
weekends are my own and I make the most of them, cooking
for friends, going horse riding and going on spa breaks at least
once a month. It's just that sometimes it all seems a little
boring. Everything is so routine, so well-ordered that
sometimes I want to break free of it all: tell my boss what I
really think of her; go travelling and not wash my hair for a

month; get off my head at a party full of people ten years my junior. I guess that was how I got myself into this mess.

It was two weeks and three days ago that it all started. I'd been at a work dinner and had indulged in a few too many glasses of wine: the client kept topping up my glass and it seemed rude to refuse. I decided to walk home to help clear my head. It was only a short journey and the streets were well lit. I ambled along, looking at the stars and enjoying the balmy evening. It felt like there was some special sparkle in the air, and when I passed the park, the swings seemed to beckon to me. I felt like being frivolous; and I had always loved playing on the swings when I was younger. Glancing around, I couldn't see anyone who'd witness my immaturity and, giggling to myself, I ran to the gates. I pushed at them but – damn – they were locked. I almost walked away, but the idea of feeling the wind whooshing past my cheeks as I swung back and forth was just too tempting. The gate wasn't that high. Hoiking my pencil skirt up to mid-thigh level, I found a foothold, gripped onto the top of the gate and clambered over it. I felt rebellious as I ran for the swings and started to play. All the stresses of my week seemed to melt away as I kicked off with ever more force, climbing higher and higher. I closed my eyes and let the elation flood my body.

"Oi! What do you think you're doing?"

The voice broke into my thoughts and I wobbled on the swing. I looked in the direction of the voice and saw a tall man in his late twenties. Reality kicked in and I realised that I was alone in a park at night with a strange man. I thought about ignoring him and hoping he'd go away but figured that would probably antagonise him. Keeping swinging so that he couldn't grab me, I answered him.

"I'm swinging."

"Well, you shouldn't be. The park's closed."

A hitherto unknown rebellious streak rose up in me, no doubt spurred on by the drink and adrenaline.

"So? It's just a bit of fun."

"And if you fell off and hurt yourself, I'd be the one who got sued. Get off the swing. You're trespassing."

With relief, I realised that he must be the park keeper.

"It's a public park."

"Only between the hours of 8 a.m. and 8 p.m. Right now, it's closed and you're breaking the law."

I slowed myself on the swing, partly because I was getting light-headed and partly because I was beginning to realise that he was right. What was I doing?

"OK, sorry. It just looked so tempting when I was walking past. I'll go now."

"Not so fast. I told you, you're breaking the law. I'm going to have to call the police."

I could see the headlines in the trade press now: 'Susie Zane arrested for playing on swings'. I'd be a laughingstock.

"Please don't," I said to the stranger. "I wasn't doing any harm. I didn't realise I was doing anything wrong."

"So you normally climb over gates to get into the park then?"

I realised he must have been watching me from the moment I entered the park.

"No, I… Oh, look, I haven't done any harm. Can't you let me go? Please?"

The stranger looked me up and down.

"Well, I might be able to let you off. But I think you need some punishment, otherwise you might do it again."

"I'll help you tidy the park. Or I could write a press release for you if you've got any events coming up here."

"Not my department. Anyway, I don't think that'd be enough punishment. No, I think you need to be taught a proper lesson."

Something in his voice made me look more closely at him. There was a definite flirtatious glint in his eyes – which, now I came to think of it, were rather twinkly and sexy.

"What do you mean?"

"I think you need a spanking."

"You what?" I was outraged at his suggestion.

"You heard me. You were acting like a naughty kid, so I think I need to treat you like one and put you over my knee."

"You pervert."

"Yes," the man said. "But only because you deserve it. If you'd prefer it, I can just call the police and let them deal with you."

I thought about my options. If the police got involved, it'd be embarrassing, not to mention a late night and I had early morning meetings to go to. If I did as the stranger asked, I'd be free to go in a few minutes and could forget about the whole sorry affair. I looked at him once more. I had to admit he was rather handsome: tall, tanned and muscular, no doubt from working outdoors all the time. He definitely had more than a touch of Alpha male about him: just my type. And it was only a spanking. The thought of feeling his hands on my pert arse made me quiver in anticipation despite myself.

"OK. But I'm not taking anything off."

"Of course you're not. So, I think fifty strokes should be fair, shouldn't it?"

"Fifty! That's ridiculous. Twenty."

"Trespass is trespass. OK, how about thirty? But you have to thank me afterwards."

I nodded my assent.

"OK, bend over this." The park keeper gestured at a climbing frame with a bar at an appropriate height. I was going to balk at the idea of being spanked in the open air but then I realised it was safer to stay in public than going into the park keeper's hut. Blushing fiercely, I bent over as indicated. I couldn't believe what was happening to me. I just hoped it would be over soon.

"Great arse," said my captor, standing back and looking at me bent over and ready for my spanking. I could feel a flush rise in my cheeks. The exposure was humiliating: even though I was fully clad, I knew that he'd be able to see my buttocks clearly outlined in my pencil skirt – and worse, the second that he touched me, he'd realise that I wasn't wearing any underwear. I heard him move closer and then – 'thwack' – his

51

hand struck my left arse cheek. I wriggled at his touch: he clearly wasn't hitting me with his full force but it still stung.

"Aren't you going to count?" he asked. "If you don't, I might forget how many times I've spanked you."

I blushed more fiercely. This really did feel like punishment.

"One."

"Very good." The park keeper spanked my right buttock as he spoke.

"Two."

"You learn quickly," he said. I could have sworn I heard him laugh but before I had a chance to think about it, he'd administered another slap to my left buttock, this time harder. I yelped in pain but had to admit that that wasn't the only sensation. To my horror, I could feel my pussy welling up. I wasn't sure if it was the humiliation or the feeling of the handsome stranger's hand on my arse but I was beginning to feel turned on.

"Three."

The next few slaps followed in rapid succession, three fierce blows to each cheek in turn. I whimpered as I kept count out loud.

"Too much for you, gorgeous? You should have been a good girl, shouldn't you."

"I *am* a good girl," I protested. "I'm *always* a good girl. Except tonight."

"Well, it's a good thing that I met you tonight then, isn't it. Otherwise I wouldn't get to punish you. And unless I'm entirely wrong, I think you're really quite enjoying it."

The stranger went back to a slow steady rhythm of spanks as he spoke, giving me enough time to feel the warmth spreading through my tender arse before he upped the pace with the next smack.

"I don't know what you mean," I hissed, even though I could feel my nipples pressing against my thin silk shirt by now, and was beginning to worry that he'd notice if he moved to look at my face. Luckily for me, he was quite happy with the view from behind.

"Don't give me all that coy nonsense. It's obvious that you're enjoying it. Hardly surprising, really. Sensual women always do."

"And what makes you think that I'm sensual?"

Even though I was angry at the assumption, I had to admit that I was also flattered.

"Well, most women wear underwear to work. You clearly like feeling the air against you. And that makes you sensual."

I was glad that it was dark so that he couldn't see my blush.

"Anyway, you've stopped counting. If you're not careful, I'll throw in a few more spanks to make sure that you behave properly in future."

He was spanking me evenly and rapidly, making my arse glow. I felt another surge of wetness to my pussy but returned my attentions to keeping count. What was happening to me? I'd never been spanked before. I'd certainly never let a stranger touch me in public before. Now both were happening and I was relishing every second of it. I deliberately said "twenty," as the stranger spanked me once more – lower than the amount of spanks I knew I'd had. I could have sworn that the next smack was just that little bit harder, but whether in punishment or reward for what I'd done, I wasn't sure.

"Spread your legs," the park keeper said, his voice husky. Even though I was nervous, I did as he asked. Smack number 21 went to my left inner thigh, and number 22 went to the same place on the right hand side. The sting to my tender skin was delicious. I knew that my juices were pooling out of me now, and that it wouldn't be long before the stranger could see the dampness on the back of my skirt. The only question was, did I want him to? My head was spinning so much that I wasn't entirely sure I'd care.

Spank number 23 returned to my arse. I thought about skipping counting, letting him know that I was enjoying what he was doing but I wasn't sure I had the courage. After all, what would that lead to? Instead, I maintained the count but didn't try to mask the arousal in my voice. The man responded by hitting harder, beating a rapid tattoo on my arse before finishing with one final viciously hard slap across both cheeks at the same time.

"Thirty." My voice rang clear but I stayed in position. I wasn't sure what I was doing: did I want him to carry on? My body said yes but the flush on my face said otherwise.

"You're free to go. Unless you don't feel you've been punished enough."

The words brought me back to reality.

"Of course I've been punished enough. I can't believe you did that, you sod."

"Yeah, yeah. Go home, good girl. Think yourself lucky that you met someone as nice as me. You could have ended up in a lot more trouble."

I stood up and walked across the park with as much dignity as I could. The man followed me.

"What are you doing?"

"Letting you out." He jangled his keys at me. "Can't have you climbing over the gate again now, can I?"

I walked home, arse stinging, thoughts of the stranger buzzing through my mind. When I got into bed, I found my hand drifting between my thighs and came hard at the thought of my punishment. I wasn't a good girl. I was very, very bad indeed.

The next day, I found my mind drifting to the stranger more than I'd have liked. I couldn't focus during a client meeting and even had to sneak to the toilets mid-morning to sate my lust. Something about the way he'd treated me combined with his cute smile and voice full of laughter had hit a nerve. By the end of the day, I knew what I had to do. I headed straight for the park then sat in the pub opposite, looking at my watch. The hours seemed to drag, even though I'd got a magazine with me. But eventually, I saw the clock face show the time I'd been craving: 8:01 p.m. I walked over to the park, looked at the locked gates and climbed over them. I could see my stranger only a few feet away but didn't look at him. Instead, I headed straight for the swings, sat down and kicked off. As I flew back and forwards, I knew that I wouldn't have long to wait long for him to join me...

How To Spank Me
by Shanna Germain

First, leave a note on the bed before you leave for work, telling me what to wear. I'll find it on your pillow when I wake up, and smile when I realize you've chosen the pleated pink mini-skirt, a white baby doll T-shirt and those bottom-hugging white panties that you bought me for my birthday, three to a package. Suggest, in your carefully crafted scrawl, that I wear heels. I'll know that you mean my three-inch high strappy black sandals, the ones that let you see my toes. In your PS, tell me that you'll be home at three, and that I'd better be ready.

Be late.

At 2.30, I will parade around the house in my skirt and heels, my nipples popping through my baby doll T. By 2.45, I'll get into position as instructed, bent over the kitchen table, my hands and elbows pressed against the wood, my ass in the air, just barely covered by my skirt and panties. By 3.00, I'll still be in position, anticipating your arrival with tingling nipples and tingling cunt. At 3.15, I'll notice the cramp in my right calf, the way that my hands are sweaty on the wood, the fact that the crevice of my underwear is soaked and sticking to my newly shaved skin. By 3.30, when you still aren't home, I'll convince myself I can't stand it any longer, that you're not coming, that I'm going to go back and put on sweats just to spite you. I'll consider masturbating, just to relieve the ache that's building up inside me.

Walk in the door at four o'clock, just as I'm about to give up, just as the heat in my panties has grown cold, just as I don't think I can stand it any longer. Step up behind me. When I turn my head to look at you over my shoulder, when I open my mouth to say something nasty about the fact that you're late, say, "Face forward." Say, "Don't speak."

Correct my position without saying a word. Straighten my hands on the wood and make sure my head is down on the table, then push my feet farther apart with your leg. Do it roughly. Flip the short skirt up over my ass, then rub your hands across the panties. Find the wet spot and dig your finger in, tease it there until I lift my ass higher in the air, already begging for it, moaning into the table.

Tell me to be quiet. Tell me that I am not allowed to make a sound until you say so. Stand to the left of me, and reach under my T-shirt and tweak my nipples, first one, then the other. With your other hand, return to rubbing the wet spot in my panties. Realise I am panting and pushing my ass toward your hand, trying to catch as much of your flesh as possible against my skin. Say, "Don't move." Then flick my clit through the material until I am bucking and bucking, unable to keep still.

Let your hand swat my butt cheek, just once, a swift stroke that catches the fleshy part of my ass and makes my head spin. When I cry out, do it again, and again. Threaten to tear off my panties and spank me naked. Tell me what a bad girl I am for wanting it so much. Wait until I'm panting, begging, sticking my ass toward you again and again, wait until I'm so wet I'm dripping into your hand, and then back off.

Make yourself a cup of coffee. Stand back and stare at my ass – positioned like two half-peaches in the air, barely covered by my dripping wet panties, just waiting for you. Sip your coffee while you ease the white fabric down over the cheeks of my ass without touching my skin.

Get undressed.

Do it slowly, so I can hear every button, every zipper, every slide of fabric over your skin. Press your skin against mine, hold my cheeks in your hand, first one then the other. Feel their juice, their heft. Moan. Tease my bare slit with your fingers. Keep doing it until I beg. Enter me with your fingers, first one, then two, three. Slide them inside me over and over until I'm fucking your hand, legs spread wide before you, my grunts and moans covering the sound of you fucking me.

This is your cue – slap the fleshy part of my ass with your palm.

Alternate. Repeat.

See the blush growing across my cheeks? This same redness is on my face too – excitement, shame, joy.

Pay attention as you spank me. Note the change in pitch when I moan, the way I toss my head back, just a little, each time your hand slaps my ass. I'm about to come.

Stop.

Step back and pick up the belt that's draped over the back of the chair. Run the leather through my wet crack and across my clit, until you feel me shiver, until I arch my back, begging for it. Tell me you'll let me have it if I touch myself. Wait until I take my hand off the table, press it between my legs, look back over my shoulder at you, begging.

Take the end of the belt and slap it, soft, against my ass. So that it makes a noise, but doesn't hurt too much yet. Let me know there's more where that came from. Ask me if I want it.

When I whisper *yes,* slap me a little harder and ask me again. When I say *yes*, slap the other side and ask me again and again, until I'm grunting *please, yes please, yes, yes, yes*, until my flesh is warm and red beneath your hand, until the sound of the belt against my ass is so loud, so much louder than my own voice as I arch and quiver and come.

Wait until I am able to breathe again, until I can back away from the table, then hug me against you so I will not fall. Tell me how much you love to make me come. Tell me that it's my turn to be on top tomorrow.

Love, Honour And Obey
by DMWCarol

The starters were carefully placed on the table just seconds before the grandmother clock in the hallway struck six. Jo smoothed out the rumples from her skirt, fluffed up her hair and prepared to welcome her husband home. It was the first night they'd had to themselves in nearly two months, the kids were at their aunties', there were no meetings or friends in need to deal with and it was going to be wonderful – she looked great, the food was ready to dish up, the makings of a bath were laid out, the sheets were pristine and there was a bottle of Chardonnay and half a dozen chocolate truffles on ice in the bedroom. Any time now Chris would be pulling up outside and she could hardly wait to reveal her surprise.

Jo poured herself a glass of wine and sank into the comfortable leather sofa, the music was soft and sensual with just enough of a beat to keep it sexy rather than sleepy, loud enough to notice, but not so loud it would hide the sound of the car pulling onto the drive. It had been a busy day, but tonight was going to make every second of preparation worth while. Still it was nice to have a few minutes to relax before her plan kicked into action.

The music really was quite erotic, by the time she'd finished her wine she was starting to feel really horny. Maybe dinner could wait a while, it wasn't anything that would spoil, she could drag him off to bed first, or maybe just pull him onto the sofa with her and save the time it would take to get upstairs. Maybe she should greet him in just the sexy new black basque, minuscule thong and the seamed stockings she'd bought for the evening, he'd always said it was the perfect way to be greeted home …

Another glass of wine and she was half naked, straining her ears for the sound of the car. It was strangely exciting waiting like this, but surely, he should have been here by now? Maybe the traffic was a bit heavy though, nothing to worry about.

It's amazing how sitting around unappreciated in your scanties after several hours of housework and cooking can dampen a mood. By the time Chris was half an hour late, the CD had needed changing and the second glass of wine was empty, Jo's mood had totally plummeted. Where the heck was he?

The waiting had stopped being exciting and was well on the way to irritating. The clock in the hall was a constant reminder of the seconds ticking past without Chris. OK, so he didn't know she was planning anything, but even so – where was he? As the clock chimed seven she moved from angry to worried, maybe something had happened? A quick ring to his mobile provided the answer – he was working late and he hadn't even had the decency to call and tell her! Jo slammed down the phone in disgust. She knew her husband did not appreciate calls at work, but he didn't have to be so damn rude. It was hardly unreasonable to want to know why he was an hour late!

Jo loved her husband, but he could be so inconsiderate at times, work always came first, especially when he was stressed. Jo was so angry she could scream. She stormed into the kitchen, dumped the dinner in the dogs' bowls, and then headed upstairs to retrieve jeans and a T-shirt.

The rotten bastard thought that all she was good for was looking after the kids, tidying the house, and cooking his dinner. He'd forgotten what it was like to be fun and naughty and young and he was trying to make her forget too. Well stuff him! She decided. And snatching up her handbag she strode out of the house and off to her best friend's house. Laurie always knew how to cheer her up.

Several cups of tea, half a pack of chocolate digestives and two chick flicks later she was not even close to cheered up. It didn't help that the second film was set in a high school and the lead character in the story reminded her of how much fun Chris used to be. They'd been friends since they were kids and it didn't seem possible that he'd gone from the naughty schoolboy everyone had wanted to be with to Mr Boring with his suit and laptop and never ending meetings and business trips.

"Maybe the naughty boy is still in there somewhere?" Laurie suggested.

"Not a chance," Jo replied. "He may have been naughty, but he was always nice back then. He'd never have treated me the way he does now. Miss Flude would have given him six of the best if he'd been this much of a swine!"

Maybe that's what he needs, she thought with a laugh. A good hiding might teach him a lesson. Six of the best right across his naughty bottom. What a pity she didn't have a cane.

She pictured Chris bent over the dining table, pants at his ankles as she administered the caning he so richly deserved. Laurie joined her in laughing at the idea. That was what she needed. A good laugh made her feel so much better. Jo hoped that Laurie hadn't noticed that the idea of punishing Chris had rekindled more than just her good mood. The way his nicely rounded arse was presenting itself in her mind was a lot more arousing than she'd have wanted even her best friend to realise.

Chris was clearing up the mess she'd left in the kitchen when Jo finally got home. She'd hung around a while letting her friend's easy humour soothe away all the anger and hurt. No need for him to know that, though! She wasn't going to let him off that easily. A whole day's work had been wasted and that image of his bare arse was provoking her to make him pay in ways they might both enjoy.

"You didn't have to be so rude to me you know, dear husband," Jo said from the kitchen doorway.

"I know. Look, I'm really sorry, I was just really busy and hadn't noticed the time. My project is at a really critical point and someone had messed up the figures," he replied, without interrupting his washing up.

"Well, I'm important too. I'd been working all day to make tonight special for us and you ruined it all. And this isn't the first time either! You've been interested in nothing but work lately and it's making you grumpy and inconsiderate. We're supposed to be partners, you know, and if you want that to continue you can stop treating me like dirt, or I might have to take some drastic measures!" Jo added ominously.

"What on earth are you talking about?" Chris demanded.

Jo dropped her voice to a husky whisper and walked over to caress Chris's arse.

"I'm a mum now, Chris." Jo breathed. "And that means that I spend a lot of time dealing with children. I know exactly how to deal with naughty boys with no manners!" Chris's face registered his shock at what she was saying. Jo lifted her hand and brought it down with a sharp slap against his bottom. "I'm sure I can deal with a naughty boy who is supposed to have grown up just as easily!" she teased

"Are you serious?" Chris asked, apparently shocked.

Jo took a step backwards. Chris stared back at her, jaw hanging and eyes wide with surprise.

"I've never been more serious!" Jo replied, giving Chris a stern glare. "If you don't treat me right, you can expect to be disciplined. You can't possibly think it is acceptable to neglect me and take me for granted as you have been doing?"

Chris shook his head, and even managed an apologetic look – although Jo was well aware that the bulge growing in his trousers was far from sorry.

"I deserve love, occasional romance and most importantly to be appreciated," Jo stated. Chris nodded his agreement. "You have ignored my needs for too long already and tonight we are going to begin to redress the balance."

Jo peeled off the jeans and T-shirt and Chris's eye almost bulged out of his head at the sexy sight this revealed. The black basque and stockings had transformed Jo into the most exotic creature. Chris was no longer looking just at his wife, but at a gorgeous sexy Amazon, full of fire and passion who could easily have stepped out of one of his most secret fantasies.

"It's rude to stare! And I've had more than enough of your bad manners for one day," Jo snapped in the haughtiest voice she could manage.

"Sorry, Mistress," Chris responded automatically, and felt his cock twitch with excitement. He was astonished at this transformation in his normally so-quiet wife. He was even more amazed at just how incredibly erotic he found her like this. She was in control, and he wasn't quite sure he knew how to deal with it.

His unthinking words gave Jo the extra confidence she needed. "You have been a very naughty boy Chris. You have been thoughtless and insensitive. You need to be taught a lesson, and as your loving wife and the mother of your children I shall be the one to deliver your punishment. You will be made to share the pain that your lack of consideration has caused. As my lesson to you, I intend to spank your bare bottom until it is as red as the roses you will be buying me tomorrow to accompany your apology. I will be as hard on you as your neglect has been on me. This will hurt a great deal."

Chris found Jo's words disturbingly erotic, but also frightening. If he went through with this things could change for ever between them, but could he get out of it?

"You are going to be spanked for behaving like a selfish schoolboy. Don't you have anything to say for yourself?" Jo asked.

"Um. I didn't mean to upset you," Chris replied weakly.

"Too late, Chris," Jo said with a shake of her head "Now bend over the table and make yourself ready."

When Chris didn't respond instantly Jo grabbed his arm and twisted it behind him before marching him to the table. He struggled and protested, but Jo paid no attention.

"Enough!" She snapped. "You have earned your punishment and you are going to take it whether you want to or not. Now bend over," Jo wasn't sure where the strength came from, but she pushed on his back and Chris found himself bent submissively over the desk.

"Now we are going to bare that bottom of yours," Jo said and made short work of undoing his pants and sliding them down to his knees. She flipped the bottom of his shirt up above his waist and stepped back to enjoy the view she had been imagining all evening.

The reality was every bit as sexy as she'd imagined. Chris's face was bright red but his cock was as hard as the wood of the table. She wondered how she had never noticed before just how much his sweet white bottom was crying out for a vibrant red palm print, or several.

"You are to stand perfectly still, understood?"

"Yes, Mistress," Chris replied, his voice almost a squeal.

"This is not going to be easy on you, but you really need this. You have earned every single stroke."

Jo raised her hand high, then brought it down hard on the left cheek of Chris's bottom.

Smack!

Chris winced as he felt the burning sensation flare across his bottom. Again and again her hand swept down on him. It took a while for her to get the hang of it, but soon blows were raining one on top of the other and the burning was growing stronger and stronger.

Jo paused for a few seconds and changed the stroke to a gentle caress, Chris whimpered then howled as she immediately switched back to the heavier slaps.

Swish … Smack … Swish …!

"Yow!" Chris felt that his arse was on fire. He clutched at the desk, using every ounce of will to stay still as Jo had demanded while she laid into him. Jo added to his discomfort with a litany of his faults.

"A good husband does not forget to call." Thwack!

"A good husband comes home on time." Slap!

"A good husband remembers to say thank you." Smack!

"Ow!" Chris cried out. His bottom felt completely raw, but his cock was so hard he was sure it was damaging the table. "Thank you, Mistress!" he whimpered. "Thank you for showing me the error of my ways." His words caught Jo off guard. "I'll do better," he promised, "I'll be the husband you deserve."

"Really?" Jo asked, slowing the onslaught to add a few gentle caresses in between the blows. "You haven't been very good so far," she mused. "But then, now you know you can expect to be disciplined if you fail me, I imagine it will be easier to remember your manners."

Her hand snaked between his legs to test the rigidity of his cock. "I don't suppose it will be hard to remember at all," she said as she gripped his shaft and gave it a confident squeeze. "But if you do forget you know what will happen don't you?" A last stinging blow rammed her message home.

"No, Mistress!" Chris whimpered as his knees weakened and he sank to the floor.

Jo kicked him onto his back and surveyed the effects her spanking had had on him with a critical eye. He was shocked and sore but not broken, but he was already looking at her with new respect.

For a second her instincts told her to comfort him and tell him it would all be alright, but this was not the night for half measures and she quickly shook the impulse away.

"You are going to be very, very good to me in future," she told Chris as she stepped out of her thong. "And you can start right now," she declared as she straddled him and pulled his face towards her waiting pussy.

And he was.

Don't Mess With The Dean
by Eva Hore

'Okay, Brad. I'll see you tomorrow then,' I gushed, as he kissed my cheek.

Closing the door behind me, I waited until I heard his car take off before breathing a sigh of relief. He was so boring. I was only dating him to please my parents. Since enrolling at this University, he wouldn't leave me alone. He was the son of an old friend of my parents, Mr Carney, our Dean. Ugh!

I could just hear the low volume of a television set and a murmuring voice as I let myself into the apartment. Oops, my flat-mate Sarah must have company, I thought. Her bedroom door was slightly ajar and, being nosey, by nature I decided to take a peek, see who she was entertaining in there.

I sidled along the wall until my eye was peering through the crack in the door. She was lying in the middle of the bed, naked, her legs splayed open and masturbating. I tried to see if there was anyone else with her but I could only see her.

A loud slap reverberated through her room as she slapped at her pussy. I almost gasped out loud, I was so surprised. I'd never seen anyone do that before. She rolled over and I got a great shot of her creamy arse cheeks staring back at me. A buzzing noise and then a big black dildo came into view.

'You like to watch, don't you?' she said.

Someone was in there with her. Who, I wondered? I knew I should go to my room, stop spying on her but I couldn't tear myself away. I wanted to see what else she would do and more importantly what the other person would do to her.

Barely breathing, I watched as she slipped the dildo between her gaping flaps. Mesmerized by the sight of the black monster as it pounded her pretty pink pussy, I found my own pussy throbbing, wanting some attention. I was desperate to go to the privacy of my own room, desperate for some masturbation as well.

'Bring your cock over here,' she demanded. 'I want to suck you off.'

'No,' a voice said.

Who was that?

'Oh, please,' she begged.

'Rub your clit,' he demanded.

Who was that? His voice sounded vaguely familiar. I watched as she pulled the hood back over her clit and began to rub. I'd never seen another woman naked like this before and found it was turning me on.

'Now finger-fuck yourself, you little slut,' he said.

'I want you to fuck me,' she pouted.

'Do as I say.'

She inserted a few fingers and began to thrust in and out of herself, rising up, her breasts falling as she lowered her eyes to watch herself. Then she was back at her clit, rubbing hard and fast. She fell back, her back arching, her breasts straining forward, nipples erect while her breath came out in gasps.

'Oh, yes, yes,' she squealed. 'I'm … I'm coming.'

'Stop!' he ordered.

She didn't though: she kept right on rubbing, her body thrashing about the bed as she came. She lay back exhausted, eyeing him through hooded lashes. What was she up to now?

'Didn't I tell you to stop?'

She pouted at him.

'You know I'll have to punish you now, don't you?'

She giggled stupidly.

'Roll over.'

She did eagerly, eyeing him over her shoulder.

A rustling of clothing had my senses alerted. I was ready to run in case I got caught. An arm came into view, and then a back and a hairy arse. It was an older man; the back of his hair was receding.

In his hand he had a ruler.

'Up on all fours,' he said.

She wiggled her arse at him and he slapped her with the ruler.

'Ow,' she cried.

'Quiet,' he said, slapping at her thighs.

I watched mesmerized as welts formed on her flesh. Criss-crossed markings covered her arse and thighs. Lowering his head he seemed to be kissing them, his hand rubbing over the rawness, the ruler now discarded.

'You like being bad, don't you?' he asked.

'No,' she whimpered.

'But you like being spanked don't you?'

'No, sir, I don't.'

Sir? Why did she call him that?

'Roll over and spread your legs for me.'

She did.

Slipping a finger inside her, he chuckled. 'You loved it alright. You're wet, very, very wet.'

'Well, maybe just a little,' she giggled.

'Let's see if you taste as good as you feel.'

He knelt on the floor before her, grabbed her by the hips and pulled her forward. Opening her legs he held them wide while she whimpered for him to hurry. Lowering his head, he began to lick her pussy, lifting her legs high so they hung over his shoulders and flopped about.

'Very nice indeed.'

'Oh, God, yes, that's fantastic,' she whispered.

Shit, for an old guy he certainly knew how to please her. She was wild, whimpering as she pushed her pelvis into his face. She pulled the hood back over her clit and began to rub like crazy while he nuzzled to munch on her.

Then he climbed up onto the bed and into her open thighs. Her legs wrapped themselves around his back, drawing him down. She squealed as his cock speared into her. I watched them humping, her heels kicking into his back as she spurred him on.

'Oh, yes, fuck me. Fuck me harder, harder,' she begged.

He slammed into her and I swear the floor shook with the ferocity of the pounding he was giving her. His arse cheeks clenched and contracted as he pummelled her. My hand found its way into my own panties, running over my slit. I parted the lips, slipped a finger in and began to finger myself. My panties were restricting me so I quietly slipped them off.

Now I could really attack my clit. Smearing my silky juices over my hardened nub I rubbed frantically, pleased when I felt the spasms taking over and my juices begin to flow more freely. Peering back in on them I saw they'd changed positions, that she was up on all four, doggy style and he was slamming her from behind, slapping at her arse cheeks in the process.

'Oh,' she whimpered. 'That hurts.'

'I told you if you didn't do everything exactly how I said, I'd have to give you another spanking.'

'But I did. I did everything you told me to.'

'Quiet,' he demanded. 'You're being disobedient and for that I'll have to spank you properly.'

He pulled his dripping cock from her and smacked her hard on the cheek, leaving the imprint of his hand. The other welts were still there but not quite as visible. She squealed and he slapped harder. In no time her cheeks were bright red. Then he was caressing them, rubbing lovingly before slapping at her thighs.

'Please, no more,' she said.

'Does this hurt?' he slapped at her again.

'No.'

'No? Does that mean I've been easy on you? That I haven't applied as much pressure as I should?'

How could she say no, I wondered? Her arse was bright red, her thighs had matching welts. Why was she allowing him to do this? Sarah was a bit of a prude, always on her high horse about equality for the sexes, women's rights and all that.

He picked up the ruler he'd discarded.

'You ready for another spanking?' he said.

'Yes, I am. I'm sorry for not doing what I was told. Please spank me.'

Never in my wildest dreams would I have thought that she'd be into this sort of stuff.

As he began to administer the punishment, the ruler slapping rhythmically, I had the most powerful of orgasms. It was amazing. I'd never had one like that before. I wondered if it had something to do with the spanking, if perhaps I too would enjoy it, enjoy someone slapping me, making it sting like fire.

He didn't use the ruler for too long. Sarah went wild, thrashing herself around the bed, lunging for his cock, begging him to fuck her. By now she had some blue marks, obviously he was spanking her quite hard with the ruler and before spearing himself into her saturated cunt, he lowered his head and licked the injured areas lovingly.

Now the real pounding began. She was screaming and flinging herself around while he called her every filthy word you can imagine. I was dripping. Watching them had me coming, one orgasm after another. It took all my willpower not to go in and join them.

For an old guy he was incredible. He had the stamina of a man much younger. I was just about to come when the phone in the hallway rang. I froze and so did they. He looked over his shoulder toward the door and my heart stopped.

It was Mr Carney. She was fucking Mr Carney. I couldn't believe my eyes. I held my breath as the phone rang out and they resumed their lovemaking. I crept back to the front door and outside, trying to quiet my hammering heart. The wind had picked up and it whistled passed my naked snatch.

No wonder she had called him sir!

Where had I left my panties? Oh, no! outside Sarah's door. I didn't know what to do, go back or hope they didn't see them. I sat on the bench, pulling my skirt around my thighs while I pondered what to do.

In about half an hour, while still sitting on the bench, a shadow passed over me. I looked up to see Mr Carney. We eyed each other, neither of us speaking. He dropped my panties in my lap.

'I believe these are yours,' he said.

'Er ...' what could I say?

'Sarah has an early class tomorrow. I believe spying on your flat mate is against the rules and you know what that means, don't you? If you're interested in receiving your punishment leave your door unlocked. I'll see you at seven.'

He walked off, confident and sure of himself, knowing after what I'd witnessed that there'd be no way I'd say no. My bum was twitching, wondering what it would be like to be spanked. I couldn't wait for tomorrow to come.

His Lordship's Satin Knickers
by Virginia Beech

Lord Camberley whipped a final cut across the rounded cheeks of maid Gloria's now reddened and quivering bottom and lowered the rattan cane. He looked across at his German Housekeeper Freja and Butlerine Cordelia, who were holding the new maid down by her wrists over his tooled leather desktop. Flushed with anticipation for what they knew was to follow as they surveyed maid Gloria's glowing globes twitching sensually before them, they noted the nascent erection straining within his tight riding breeches. The noble cock of the Master of the Camberley Foxhounds was throbbing lustily within its strict confines of Gieves cavalry twill, a heated animal aroused by the caning and desperate to be freed.

Housekeeper and Butlerine had prepared maid Gloria well for this sensual punishment scene now being played out on a warm June evening in the Master's Study, knowing she would find ecstasy in the pain and joyfully humour the rampant one-eyed beast when it was let loose from its trousered cage.

Camberley paused to enjoy the rousing spectacle causing such turmoil within his breeches. Maid Gloria's lushly plump and dimpled spheres were still quivering from his cane's final stroke. It had been the hardest cut, bringing a throaty grunting intake of breath from her lips as she mouthed the strike as instructed by Freja, who was acting as Mistress of Ceremonies for this, the first of what she intended to become a regular seance attended by the Earl, butlerine and the maid she had chosen to join the household at Camberley House, No.63 Grosvenor Square.

The appointment of Fraulein Freja von Hohenfels, the tall, handsomely well-endowed, flaxon haired Nordic Domina as his new Housekeeper at the April start of the 1882 London season, changed the life of both the Earl of Camberley and the beautiful Cordelia, his long-suffering butlerine. The Prussian dominatrix hired from Berlin had quickly spotted Hubert's particular fetishist tastes; a partiality for buttocks and cane, satin knickers and masturbation. Having first abstracted Cordelia's bottom from the first part of this equation by taking her to her bed as lover and confidante, Freja set about providing the Earl with satin knickers to don and masturbate in and then caned his bottom for being such a "naughty boy"; a satisfactory arrangement for all concerned. The knickers were hers and inspiringly impregnated with the deliciously feminine fragrance of Freja's sapphic lovemaking with Cordelia. Satin knickers and orgasmic release followed by a spanking over Freja's knee, soon became a natural progression of delight for Hubert.

Between them, Freja and Cordelia soon had Camberley yielding to a complicit role reversal. Master was becoming slave. By June, Housekeeper Freja was Mistress of Camberley House in all but name. In keeping with her *de facto* status she moved downstairs from the cramped servant's quarters and settled herself with Cordelia in the palatial suite overlooking the square on the 2nd floor above the ballroom. She began to arrange her mornings to be seen elegantly attired, cantering side-saddle down nearby Hyde Park's fashionable Rotten Row as she exercised Hector, the Earl's handsomely groomed, high-stepping thoroughbred stallion at the 11 o'clock social hour. Decorum required that she be suitably chaperoned on such occasions and Cordelia looked stunning in that capacity. London society began to take notice.

It was on just such a morning, while they were pausing at

Hyde Park Corner where the Row and South Carriage Drive meet in a social whirl of equestrian finery and expensive uphostery, that Gloria had approached them and begged for alms. The upshot of this meeting was that half an hour later she was ensconced behind Cordelia on her horse trotting up Park Lane to a new life at Camberley House.

Gloria's story was typical of many young ladies of this period. Turned out of home as 'fallen women', these unfortunates thronged London's West End where they begged or sold their bodies to survive. Gloria's penchant for the meaty cock of the local blacksmith in the small Hertfordshire village, where her father was a fiery preacher and she the supposedly prim village schoolteacher, had been her particular undoing. Discovered by the blacksmith's wife in his hayloft enjoying a satisfying bare bottom spanking over her naked husband's muscled knee, having milked him of the cumcream properly belonging to her, Gloria had been promptly disowned as a whoring Jezebel by her embarassed father ("Never darken my door again!"), and forced to flee the wife's wrath. Her story, peaches-and-cream complexion, curvaceous posterior and proven pleasure in baring it for suitable chastisement, won this English Rose with winsome smile and silver-throated laugh a niche position in the Camberley household. Freja and Cordelia had found the dainty derriere that would titillate their nominal master and amuse them!

The grooming of maid Gloria for such a sensual role had been remarkably easy. She proved to be adept, agile and adventurous on her back and suitably submissive on her knees. Her kama-sutric appetite was insatiable, her laughter infectious and her tears enchanting. She took to the sapphic delights of deep tongue caressing as a duck takes-to-water and it was not long before Domina Freja collared her as their willing and submissive Handmaiden.

Lord Camberley knew nothing of his Housekeeper's preparation of additional erotic pleasures that would further ensnare him within her satin-knickered web, until maid Gloria was presented at his study for punishment, having allegedly broken a piece of Sevres porcelain dinner service and failed to inform the Butlerine. It was the first time he had set eyes upon her and, dressed in the satins of slutmaidenly uniform, she was what he would describe as a "toothsome morsel". His monocled eye lit up. He twirled his handlebar moustaches, grunted approvingly and snorted a pinch of aromatic Kendal Brown snuff. The spider had caught her fly! The time was ripe for Freja to display Gloria's delectable derriere for noble approbation before stuffing her pink pouting lips with the noble meat of blue-blooded sausage!

Freja and Cordelia set the scene for maid Gloria's flagellation debut by first positioning her over the Earl's study desk. Freja invited him to pull the black satin skirt of her uniform up over her back to reveal her posterior enclosed in tight fitting white satin knickers. They required firm coaxing from the Earl's trembling hands to persuade them to relinquish their hold on her shapely hips. He pulled them slowly down to bare her rounded bottom cheeks so invitingly framed by black sateen corset and white silk stockings stretched over her thighs by straining suspender tabs. Positioned now with knickers tautly stretched at her knees she presented a picture of helpless sensuality that had Hubert Camberley salivating in anticipation.

Housekeeper picked up two suede floggers and handed one to Butlerine.

'We shall now prepare maid Gloria's posterior for your caning by first flogging her, my Lord. Please count the strokes!'

It was a sensual warm-up. They wielded the floggers alternately with a slow, measured pace bringing a blushing glow to the sweet cheeks posed provocatively before them. The lashes packed little sting but provided considerable visual titillation, landing with a satisfying thud; a sensual spanking of 100 strokes that brought intense pleasure to the recipient. Playing to the lascivious lusts of the noble Master of the House, maid Gloria bucked, writhed and squealed enticingly as the thudding tails caressed her beautiful bottom. After the first 50 strokes she lapsed into a dreamy silence that verged on euphoric trance.

It was the perfect preparation for his Lordship's rattan. Despite his trembling excitement, he managed to wield his cane with firm precision to maid Gloria's heated and receptive cheeks, raising fiery crimson welts that would later cool to warm shades of indigo and purple. The strokes stung deeply, cutting across the suffused blushes left by the flogging and bringing a delirious rush of adrenaline and endorphines to the pinioned maid. She screamed at both the pain and the thrill of each stroke. Her bottom felt as if it was on fire and she felt a telltale moistness between her parted legs.

Maid Gloria's plump lovelips nestling within their rich oval of blond curls were only partially concealed by the luscious curve of her now enflamed globes. She wriggled, hoping her caner would see her arousal. Lord Camberley bent forward and probed her slit gently with his long middle finger. A quiver coursed through her body, her soft wet cuntlips parting at his touch, moistly inviting his finger to seek her clitoris, now hard, throbbing and begging for relief.

Camberley felt a flowing moistness on his hand as maid Gloria squirmed to take his probing finger deeper inside her. He found and rubbed the stiffened clit that stood sentinel above the silken portal to her wet vagina. The slippery juices of her aroused pussy sucking at his probing finger brought an anticipatory quiver from Camberley's imprisoned cock. Today he would enjoy facefucking maid Gloria's beautiful and voluptuously sensual mouth.

The Earl caressed the tortured heat of her delectable posterior for a moment, feeling the maid wriggle against his hand and savoring the vision of hot stripes now glowing upon the smooth roundels of her twitching bottom. He looked at his Housekeeper and saw the approving nod he was hoping for. He began to unbutton his breeches.

"Your bottom discipline is complete for today. Turn and kneel before his Lordship!" Freja commanded.

Maid Gloria looked over her shoulder. Her eyes opened

wide and a flush suffused her face as she saw his unleashed cock burst from its tight constraints to stand forth in noble glory. It looked enormous to her fascinated gaze; 10 inches of rigid, throbbing manhood pointing upwards in a demanding and splendidly lustful erection that surpassed even that of her blacksmith lover.

Freja let go of her wrist. "Remember your lessons in maidenly conduct, Gloria! What are your duties?"

"A maid must abase herself before the Master after bottom discipline and seek to give him every pleasure he may desire," she whispered, remembering the rules Freja had drummed into her at the point of her dildo.

"Master exerted himself considerably in taking his cane to my naughty bottom and I humbly thank him for his consideration."

"Stand and adjust your dress! Turn and kneel before that beautiful cock!" Freja commanded. She and Cordelia looked lasciviously at Camberley's monstrous protuberance. Although cocks were not to their particular sapphic taste, they admired the aesthetics of its size and beauty, knowing that their debutante in this party would enjoy making a meal of such a monumental offering. Happy to remove her flaming bottom from the prospect of further stinging cuts from the Earl's cane, maid Gloria stood up and pulled up her dropped knickers to cover her posterior and dripping cunt. She smoothed her satin uniform back down over her curvaceous thighs and tummy, aware that it was heavily creased from her excited twisting and turning during her flogging, caning and Lord Camberley's pussy probing expedition.

Maid Gloria turned and knelt before His Lordship's throbbing phallus as if to worship before its magnificence. She was unprepared for the purple monster erection thrusting six inches before her face and she wondered with awe whether her mouth could accommodate such a rigid thickness and length. His weapon stood erect and pulsating, exuding a golden dribble of pre-cum.

Freja and Cordelia came round and stood behind the

kneeling maid. Bending over her, each put a hand into her bodice and removed her full pendulous breasts to hang free; voluptuous firm globes with puffy pink aureoles and large nipples. Cupping the fullness of her heavy breasts they felt the nipples harden to their touch. They teased and squeezed the erect buds as they had so often done in their nightly fuck and suck orgies, kneading maid Gloria's tits tantalisingly in front of the Earl's slavering gaze. The girls and maid Gloria knew they would be sucking her hard nipples long after the Earl had retired for the night.

"Take the Master's proffered 'person' with proper deference!" Freja commanded in a low voice. Mesmerized, maid Gloria stretched out a hand to touch its warm satiny texture. She drew her tongue provocatively over her moist mouth, feeling its virile heat and blood-engorged head pulsating excitingly between her fingers. The adrenaline was pumping again as she felt the throbbing veins of his hot lance in her hand.

"Take his Lordship's balls out of his breeches!"

Freja spoke huskily. Despite herself, her own nipples were hardening and her cunt creaming at the seductive thrill of maid Gloria's enactment of the unfolding scene and knew that Cordelia was equally aroused by the mounting tension of the moment. Maid Gloria groped into the Earl's breeches, searching delicately for his hidden balls. She tingled at their warm touch, pulling them reverently out to hang free beneath his erect weapon. Fascinated, she cupped their firm roundness in her hand, delighting in their weight. They felt enormous and swollen in their virility, heavy like the ivory billiard balls in the Earl's Smoking Room. She ran her serpentine tongue down the length of his cock to take one in her mouth and sucked it appreciatively, revelling in its warm round smoothness.

Freja bent to maid Gloria's ear. "Caress his balls with your hand and suck that hot cock the way I taught you with my dildo," she whispered. You learned to suck cunt in our bedroom. Now show us how you sucked that blacksmith's cock!"

Maid Gloria needed no admonition. Her breath was coming in short pants. She thrust her upturned breasts further out, encouraging her friends to squeeze her nipples even harder. She gave a throaty growl of desire as the pain from her tortured tits raced through her body to arouse her clitoris in masochistic delirium. She licked her lips with her long tongue and then sucked at his hot purple cockhead, tentatively at first, savoring the sweetness of his pre-cum. Then, with a throaty gurgle, she closed her lips avidly over the mushroom, probing and exploring its satiny texture until her tongue found its tiny tender-nerved aperture.

The Dominatrix in Freja was now strongly aroused. "Suck! Suck it! Suck it hard! Suck it deep, just as you do when you have your pretty slutface slurping at my cunt or sucking Cordelia's clit!" she hissed, forcing maid Gloria to take the full length of cock in her mouth and bringing her to a frenzy. Her lips closed over the hot meat, her teasing tongue sliding easily down the thick shaft as she began to suck. Its heat filled her mouth as her lips commenced their sensual pumping massage; pink lips gliding to and fro, sliding up and down the cock's glistening rigidity. She gurgled huskily as she maneuvered the enormous mushroom head ever deeper down her throat. I'm Mistress Freja's slutslave, she thought deliriously, and I love this cock as Mistress Freja knew I would. Her own cunt was deliciously wet and throbbing with desire for Freja's hot tongue. She released Camberley's swinging balls and slid a hand down inside the tight satin of her knickers to rub her heated clit while frigging cock the way Mistress had demonstrated to her the previous night with a dildo.

Maid Gloria sensed the Master's approaching orgasm quicken to her rhythm. His juices were rapidly rising as she feverishly frigged, fondled and feasted. The pulsating energy of his excitement filled her receptive mouth. Saliva oozed from between her lips, dribbling over his heated shaft.

"Harder!" he grunted, "Harder! Milk me! Suck hot spunk

while I fuck your cuntface and squeeze your big tits, or I'll whip your bitch-ass again!"

She redoubled her efforts. He rammed his cock in, hard against the back of her throat, withdrawing to the tip of its wet glistening glans, before thrusting back again to be enveloped between those luscious lips, his balls slapping rhythmically against her chin.

An explosive force was building in his taut flat stomach. An ocean of semen began its rise in a quivering jerking crescendo of nerve power. It swelled up from his balls, pumped up through his thick shaft by his fellatrice's powerful cocksucking.

He could hold it no longer. With a sharp intake of breath, he gripped maid Gloria's head in quivering spasms. His cock exploded in a shuddering, blinding orgasm, ejaculating spurt after hot spurt of liquid pearl into her mouth. Maid Gloria gagged on the copious jets, swallowing hard to contain the seemingly endless flow of creamy spunk. It spewed out between her lips, dripping onto her heaving bosom. She smoothed the cumcream over her bare breasts like a priceless lotion till they glistened.

Camberley's legs trembled from the ecstatic fury of his stand-up facefuck. He was panting with exhaustion from his efforts. A final orgasmic tremor shot though him as he pulled his cock free to pump the last hot cumdribble onto maid Gloria's upturned face. A pearly stream of semen coursed down her nose to a passion-flared nostril. With a moan of pleasure, she took the steaming prick in her mouth again to give its mushroom head a final suck, milking the last drop before cupping the warm roundness of his balls. She nuzzled her cheek against them, kissing the jewels in an effort to rekindle his exhausted ardour.

Maid Gloria's neatly coifed long blond tresses had been dislodged by the Earl's orgasmic frenzy and hung dishevelled in wanton abandon about her shoulders, back and naked breasts. She toweled his flaccid penis and balls with the locks of her silken hair before tucking his jewels reverently back into his breeches.

She looked up with glazed, sated eyes.

"It was an honor to serve you, my Lord. My body is yours to whip whenever your Housekeeper and Butlerine decide I need to be punished."

Lord Camberley looked down at her beautiful upturned face. Such attention to household discipline deserved to be rewarded. He bent and imparted a brief kiss of acknowledgement upon her forehead. He turned and walked over to the sideboard, poured himself a stiff brandy and gave the glass a splash of soda from the gazolene while his Housekeeper helped the maid adjust her 'deshabille' and tucked her sticky breasts back into her bodice.

Maid Gloria curtsied before being led from the study.

Outside, Freja smiled triumphantly to Cordelia and gave maid Gloria a loving kiss.

"You were brilliant! We shall have our noble Lord eating out of your pussy after such a performance! I shall join you later and help Cordelia massage those nasty stripes on your pretty butt....and massage those parts which a cane cannot reach! But first, take your knickers off and hand them to me! I have some unfinished business with the Earl. My pleasure - his pain!"

"Cordelia will take you up to our suite and pamper you with a well earned perfumed bath to rid yourself of any lingering mementoes of that man before we play tonight!"

She gave maid Gloria's tender rump a proprietory pat, stuffed the maid's still warm knickers into her bodice and re-entered the study.

Freja shut the heavy study door and turned the key. There was a triumphantly predatory gleam in her eye as she looked at the agitated Earl now sitting at his desk.

"Little boys rise when Mistress enters the room. Come out from behind that desk and stand before me!

"Yes Mistress!"

Hubert came and stood before her. His breeches were still partly undone and his clothing in disarray from his earlier preoccupation.

"Hubert has been a very naughty boy! He has been exposing himself to maid Gloria and playing with her pussy. There is a mess on his breeches. We can't allow such behavior. Mr Smack will pay a painful visit to naughty Mr Bottom!"

She sat down on the leather armchair, hitched up her skirt to bare her silk-stockinged thighs and motioned to the Earl.

"Take down your breeches and bend over my knee. Mistress will give you a sound spanking, while you confess your salacious misdeeds."

Freja waited while the Earl unbuttoned himself, dropped his breeches and stepped out of them. He was wearing a pair of blue satin knickers trimmed with lace that barely hid the bulge of his prick and balls. I see you are wearing the knickers I gave you when I last spanked you. They were to remind you of your iniquitous behaviour and cure you of the sort of dirty, disgusting, degrading turpitude you displayed today. But they have obviously had no effect. And I see you have soiled them with something quite unmentionably horrid! Dirty boy!"

She pulled the satin garment down to his knees.

"A 'smack bottom' is too good for you. A good caning is what you need, and if my knickers are not enough to cure you of such filthy thoughts, I fear I must degrade you further by dressing you up beneath your hunting gear with my silk stockings and one of Mme Isadora's restrictive corsets."

Mistress's words had an immediate and rousing effect upon Hubert's cock which had been slumbering after its recent exertions. It twitched, jerked and rose to rigid attention before her at the prospect of caning and corset from Mistress.

She got up, smoothed down her skirt and walked over to the desk. Picking up the rattan lying there by the two floggers, she flexed it.

"I must obviously prescribe some of your own medicine for your buttocks, my young Hubert Camberley. You come right here to me!" She tap-tap-tapped the desktop imperiously.

As he hobbled over to the desk, Mistress took maid

Gloria's knickers from her bodice and waved them under his nose.

"Place these over your head and bend over the desk with your legs apart and present your bottom for punishment! You may smell maid Gloria's pussy perfume while I cane you. It will be a salutary reminder of your depravity."

Hubert positioned himself as his dominatrix instructed; knicker-covered head on the desktop, arms outstretched. Effectively blindfolded by the satin knickers, the Earl's senses swam with the fragrance of maid Gloria's cunt. It was a heady perfume.

Mistress's shoe kicked at his feet, forcing him to open his legs wider to stretch the knickers around his ankles taut.

She picked up a flogger.

Soft suede tails slid sensuously over his buttocks and up the crease of his splayed arse. Leather flicked sharply between his legs, suede tentacles curling around his dangling testicles to attack his throbbing penis, slapping upward at his underbelly.

There was silence for what seemed like eternity.

The grandfather clock in the hall outside whirred and began to strike six o'clock.

"Beg! Hubert! Beg me to chastise you!" Mistress's command cut through the silence.

"Please cane me, Mistress! Cane me for my depraved desires!"

Mistress put down the flogger and picked up the cane again. She took her stance, paused and swung her arm.

Whack!

The Earl grunted, his butt twitching from the stinging pleasure of the first cut. It left an angry thin red line that transmitted its nerve-exploding message to his cock which pulsed in spontaneous reflex.

Warming to her task, the Prussian Dominatrix began to lay a crimson pattern of parallel stripes across the exposed spheres before her.

Whack! Whack! Whack!

She paused between each stroke to survey its mark and run

her hand over Hubert's buttocks, caressing the heat of each raised welt as it appeared.

Whack! Whack! Whack!

The crack of each impacting cut and the ecstasy of pain each searing imprint brought, together with the heady incense of maid Gloria's cuntjuices excited the Earl to new heights of euphoric ecstasy.

Whack!

Mistress's final stroke cut viciously across the soft underside of Hubert's buttocks; the fabled 'sweet spot'. It was the defining cut that released his floodgates. He tore the knickers from his head and with a groan of delight wanked himself to spurting orgasm into their shiny folds.

The study door closed silently behind Mistress Freja von Hohenfels as she left Lord Hubert Camberley to his solitary pleasure.

The School Reunion
by Kitti Bernetti

Jeanie'd only been waiting for this moment for twenty years. As she walked up the road to the school, it gave her goosebumps even now. The happiest days of your life. Well, maybe to some but not to Jeanie.

It's amazing how some people change, she thought, catching a glimpse of her thirty-year-old self in the window of a shop. Take her for instance. As a ten-year-old, she hadn't shown much promise either in the way she looked or her intellect. She was one of the average kids as far as brains were concerned. As far as looks went, she was one of the ones the mothers outside the school gates would look at and think, 'shame'. Jeanie could see the sympathy in their eyes as their pretty, bouncy kids frolicked with the other chosen ones. She'd look at the floor and feel guilty for taking up space. Childhood hadn't been her finest hour.

But the gods had made up for it since. Once she got to thirteen, her hormones kicked in producing breasts that had developed faster than the blush on a schoolboy's cheek. Firm as a tightly blown up balloon, with nipples that stood out like thimbles, they'd been obscene, even under her thick school jumper. As if to make up for the misery of her early years, nature bestowed its kindest charms on the teenage Jeanie. Lustrous thick blonde hair so long it grazed her waist, legs the length of telegraph poles and an arse so mobile men were mesmerized by it. But the older Jeanie was even better, for she had added a touch of class.

She looked good tonight and she knew it. Jeanie had chosen her outfit well, because she knew he was going to be there and, whatever happened, she had to have him. She smiled at the reflection of her arse bobbing along. What man could resist that? Not many. Her white skirt was made of that clingy jersey that kisses every curve of a well-built woman. Close observation revealed the tiny thong hugging her hips. The plain black top she wore above it pretended to be prim but, all the while, the ardent observer could peer at it and see the roundness of an overfull cleavage poking through. One button left open at the top, and two at the bottom to reveal a tanned flat stomach, should hook her prey. It was going to be one special night. She felt her breasts tingle just at the thought of it.

As she entered the crowded hall there was that unmistakable whiff of cabbagey school dinners combined with sweat and the rubber of plimsolls. She wrinkled her pert little nose with distaste. Instantly one of the male staff members approached her. He was young, good-looking. Under different circumstances, she would have sparked with approval. But not tonight.

'Hi, what was your year?' he schmoozed.

'That would be telling. Just as a lady doesn't tell her age, she doesn't tell which years she was at school. It would be too easy to work out the vital statistics.'

'Especially for me. Let me introduce myself. Lee Sheffield, I teach maths here.'

'Lucky you,' she smirked.

'Can I show you around? Or get you a drink, maybe?' His attention was flattering. It was a shame to waste him but she had bigger fish to fry. She trawled around instead looking for the object of her desire. He wasn't in this mob. 'Is the reunion taking place just in this hall or is it spread around the school?'

'Next door as well, in the science wing.' *Of course. That was where he'd be.*

'Thanks, I know where that is.' As she made to move off,

he cornered her. 'I'd really like to reminisce with you about old times.' *Wow that was a crap chat-up line but, hey, these weren't normal circumstances and that tousled hair and those faded jeans straining with muscles were pretty cute.* 'Maybe I could have your phone number?'

She hesitated. Jeanie hadn't got to senior sales exec and a six figure salary without being focussed and there was no one and nothing which was going to put her off her goal for tonight. Nevertheless, part of her success also sprung from being open to suggestions. She dug in her Louis Vuitton handbag and fished out a business card. She gave it to him, winked and slinked off, feeling his eyes burn into her jiggling rump as she walked.

As she entered the science block she spotted her target instantly. She'd know that angular stooped figure and that sharp nose anywhere. Okay, so he was twenty years older but basically it was the same model, just skinnier, and with now grey instead of brown hair. Beside him, unmistakably, stood his wife. A dessicated little rodent of a woman, Jeanie almost laughed out loud. Picking him up would be like taking candy from a baby if that dried-up female was the only item of womanhood he'd had to screw for the last two decades.

She wandered into his field of vision and could see she'd instantly caught his eye. He always was a letch. All the kids knew it. The way he used to hang around outside the gym pretending he was stopping the boys peering in at the girls undressing, when all the while he was guiltier than they were. It made the hair on Jeanie's neck stand on end.

Completely ignoring his wife, who was instantly engaged in small talk by one of the other old girls, Mr Sloane sidled up to Jeanie. 'Can I help you?'

'Maybe,' Jeanie twirled a skein of hair provocatively in her fingers and gave him her most heavy-lidded look. 'Why, you're Mr Sloane, the physics teacher, aren't you?'

'Yes. I can't quite place you though. What year was it?'

Oh no. She wasn't going to make it that easy for him. Besides, he might start to remember and get frightened away.

'Mr Sloane, wow. You're still looking so good.'

'I am?' The old letch was as flattered as a parading peacock. He straightened himself and ran a finger through his thinning hair.

'Absolutely. I'm sure old pupils come up and tell you this all the time, but, guess what, I had such a crush on you.'

'That's interesting.' He wiped a little bit of spittle from the side of his mouth. She could see the old bastard falling – hook, line and sinker.

She wrinkled her nose and toyed with the top button of her blouse. Like a dog sniffing at a bitch, his eyes lit up. 'And do you know, it hasn't weakened at all with the years. In fact, if anything I'd say it was stronger.'

He swallowed and his Adam's apple bobbed up and down. 'Really. A fine young woman like you looking at an old has-been like me.' He took her arm, all over her like a rash, and directed her towards the dark passageway which ran alongside the science block. 'Would you like to see some of our new classrooms?'

'Actually,' she giggled girlishly, hoping she wasn't laying it on too thick. 'I'd really like to visit the old lecture theatre, the one right at the top of the building where you used to do most of your lessons. I remember watching you. We could sort of re-enact how it used to be. With you on the stage, and me sitting in the audience looking up at you, wide-eyed with admiration.'

'That would be fun, my dear,' he leered. 'Let's do it.'

In the lift, she deliberately stood close to him, her shoulder almost touching his arm. He looked hot, slightly sweaty, as if he couldn't believe his luck. She had to get him ready and this confined little space was ideal for the purpose. She breathed out, her full breasts like ledges. 'Is it me, or is it really warm in here?'

His eyes strayed down, and his tongue came out of his mouth and licked his lips. 'Yes, my dear, I think it is.' Mr Sloane's eyes bulged like a goldfish's as she undid a button on her blouse exposing the black lace of her bra and the very tops of her nipples.

Jeanie looked up at him and smiled. 'I often dreamed you and I might get stuck in this lift.'

It was all he needed to make the first move. Tentatively she felt his hand slide over the rounded globes of her taut arse. 'We might get stuck in it today,' his voice was thick with desire.

'Maybe,' she said moving her legs open slightly, knowing that he wouldn't let it pass his notice. His breathing was becoming grainy now, ragged with lust.

'You have the most delectable bottom I have ever seen on a young woman.'

She stuck it out and wiggled slightly. 'I'm glad you like it. Get down on your knees and you can have a sniff.'

'Yes, there's nothing I'd like more,' he grunted, kneeling down on the floor. First he fondled both cheeks in his bony hands. Clumsily he then grasped the hem of her skirt and pulled it up, revealing the eye-filling sight of Jeanie's behind in her tiny purple thong. Her arse thrust in Mr Sloane's bristly face, and her purple suspender belt strained to hold up the flesh coloured stockings on her long shapely legs. She hoped he liked stockings because very soon, although he didn't know it, he was going to find himself tied up securely with them. He dipped his face in, roughly pulled her bum cheeks apart and sniffed, snorting like a pig.

When she felt he'd had enough to drive him insane, Jeanie pulled her skirt down and said, 'I think this is our floor. Let's go into the lecture theatre and we can have some real fun.'

He scrambled after her as she entered the double doors that led to the huge hollow room. 'This is the spotlight, isn't it?' she said, flicking on the switch and bathing the stage in light.

'You remember things well.'

'Oh yes, I remember every minute of one particular day we were in here.'

'Come with me onto the stage,' he said, 'that way I can see you better and give you what you really want.'

She winked at him, as if he was the most desirable male in

the whole human race. In her large handbag, the bamboo cane she had carefully selected for the job bumped against her leg, sharp and hard. The room was silent, you could have heard a pin drop.

Jeanie placed her handbag on the table where she could grab it easily and stood behind it, just out of Mr Sloane's reach. She tossed her blonde locks and plumped her lips, thick with shiny gloss. 'I'll bet you like to play games, don't you, Mr Sloane?'

'I don't get much chance to play nowadays. My wife is a tad cold. In fact she's as icy as Antarctica.'

'Poor you,' pouted Jeanie.

He started to edge around the table and Jeanie darted away. 'I'd like to play very much,' he grinned, his beady eyes alight with desire.

'OK then. We start with you watching.' With that, she lifted her skirt so he could see her stocking tops and her muff, and placed her hand over the front, rubbing it suggestively. He was getting satisfyingly hard, she could see, as he pressed himself against the other end of the table, the slimy toad. His tented trousers displayed a tiny wet bubble. He was nearly ready.

Slowly and deliberately, Jeanie undid her suspenders and rolled the long stockings down those endless legs. Mr Sloane's mouth dropped open.

'Come here,' she breathed.

'Anything for you my dear. Anything to please you.'

She waved the stockings at him as he came nearer then said, 'Give me your wrists, you're going to be my slave.'

'Oh God,' he crooned, 'make me serve you.'

'Take your trousers off,' she ordered.

'Yes, yes.' He fumbled with the button and the zip, pulling them hastily down. 'Now your pants, and your shirt.'

His eyes goggled at her with the sheer joy of thinking she wanted to see his spidery body. As if. He was even more repulsive naked than dressed.

The arrogant bastard obviously thought he was God's gift

standing there with a hard-on which jutted out like a pistol.

She smiled, backing away as he tried to touch her. 'No, no, just you wait, your reward will come in a while', and slid the still warm stocking over his wrists, tied them tightly, knotted them and led him to the hard metal bracket anchored into the wall on which the whiteboard was secured. It was perfect. He wouldn't get away from that, no matter how much she thrashed him.

Now was the time to get him really worked up. Bit by bit, she undid her buttons, watching his staring eyes drinking her in. In a second she was standing in her bra which barely held her ample breasts. He stood trembling before her. 'Take off your skirt,' he croaked.

She almost laughed out loud, who did he think was giving the orders here? Humour him, just for one minute more, she thought. In a moment, she was standing there in just her thong and high heels. His hands tied mercilessly behind his back, he strained forward to where she stood just out of reach.

'Come here,' he said, 'let me lick you.'

She picked up her handbag and walked over to him. He kneeled down, his face in line with her beautiful scented muff and stuck out his tongue.

'Not so soon,' she snarled backing away. A look of fright sparked in his eyes as he peered up at her from his kneeling position. His ramrod erection stayed taut with excitement.

'You don't remember who I am, do you?' She paced around him.

'So many girls pass through here, I couldn't remember them all could I?'

She brought her muff closer to his face and put down the bag with the cane nestling in it. The thought that she and only she knew it was there filled her with a feeling of power. Complete, total, utter power.

'I'll bet you remember the name Jeanie Powell, don't you?'

Mr Sloane frowned, wrinkles scarring his forehead. He moved uneasily on his knees, obviously in some discomfort. Good. 'Jeanie Powell. That does ring a … you, you're Jeanie

Powell?' The look of uncertainty turned to one of terror.

'It's coming back now, isn't it? That day, when you told me off for losing my homework. You said you wanted to make an example of me. Remember it?'

'I … yes, but you were a naughty girl, you were …'

'Shut up.' Jeanie's magnificent breasts heaved with indignation, her nipples rock hard with excitement. 'I'm not interested in hearing you justify yourself, **Mister** Sloane. I take it you remember how you told me off in front of every single person in class. How you decided to make me squirm. Remember, remember what you did?' She paced in front of him.

'Sort of.'

'Well, maybe, if you lick my shoes, you'll remember better.'

'I hardly think …'

'Do it.'

'I'm the one used to giving orders young lady.'

'Not any more,' said Jeanie and pulled out the long hard cane from her handbag. 'Lick them.'

He stared at the cane, a look of defiance in his eyes. 'No.'

Sharply, she brought the cane down on his skinny backside. As he shot forward with the pain and squealed, she noticed his prick get even bigger. 'Oh I see,' she said smoothly, 'you like that do you?'

Insolently he stayed silent. She pulled her arm back, to its longest extent and brought the cane crashing back down on his arse. It made a cracking sound that made her heart race. He was whimpering now.

'Lick my shoes.' He looked up at her, his face red with resentment and gingerly put out his tongue. 'That's it,' she cajoled, stroking his feeble little buttocks with the cane and imagining his arsehole tweaking in anticipation. His tongue darted out like a snake and licked. 'Faster.' The faster he licked, the more turned on she became. Gradually, knowing he was watching her, she pushed her finger inside her damp thong and started to whisk. 'I'll bet you'd like to stick your finger in

92

here, wouldn't you? Bet you'd like to get your tongue in too.'

His eyes lit up in anticipation. 'Bet you thought that's what was going to happen when we came up here. Trouble is, Mr Sloane,' she said, rubbing away at her clit, feeling it swell and throb, 'I remember what a foul piece of work you were. I remember standing on this stage as a poor, ungainly ten-year-old and hearing you tell everyone how ugly I was. How stupid and ungainly, how pathetic I was and how I'd never amount to anything.' As Jeanie spoke, she watched his face, an expression of mingled desire and horrified anxiety. Fingering herself and watching his dick swell almost to bursting point, she thrust her muff near him, grabbing his hair in her hand and yanking him close while her finger darted in and out. As she watched with total satisfaction, his tongue darted towards her, desperate to get a taste, but she yanked him back. In one juddering movement, she came over her busy digit and, pulling it out, wiped her sticky juices all over his face.

'Now, it's your turn.'

Again, he didn't know what to think. Again, she had him totally in her power. He struggled, his wrists rubbing red and raw. She bought the cane up again, thwack and watched both his mouth and his dick twitch. Again it came up and again, sharply on his trembling buttocks. One more should do it. Again, she pulled back, her breasts bouncing with the effort and slammed the unyielding length of bamboo against his buttocks just as his prick exploded, firing hot sticky come in a jet across the stage.

His prick jerked, and shuddered and died, shrinking back till it was almost invisible.

'I've waited a long time for that,' she said, slipping her underwear, top and skirt back on. She installed the cane back neatly in her handbag and started to walk away.

Exhausted, hardly able to speak, unutterably miserable, he cried out, 'Stop. Untie me. Please, I beg you. You can't let them find me like this.'

'Why not?' She asked, strolling away. 'That was all part of the plan.'

As she walked through the double doors which led to the lift, suddenly, she heard a quiet but distinct round of applause. There, leaning against the wall in the shadows, having seen everything through the tiny glass window in the door, was Lee Sheffield, a wicked grin on his face. Jeanie flushed pink at the discovery. Would he tell? Would she get done for assault? Would he rush in and release Mr Sloane?

'That was the best bit of theatre I've seen in a long time. Jeanie, isn't it?' She looked down and saw that his crutch was swollen with a magnificent hard-on.

She smiled a wicked smile and realised that frigging herself hadn't nearly satiated her throbbing desire. 'Are you up for some fun too?'

'Sure', he said, 'but I think we'd better go to my flat. I like to be in control when I'm around naughty little girls'. So saying, he took her bag with the cane hard inside it and led her away into the dark starless night.

No One Ever Guesses,
And No One Guesses Now
by Lana Fox

Tonight, I wear a dress that clings to me like oil. I've never felt as physical as this. When I got home, I showered with that gel – the stuff you bought in Paris last July. It smells of dry vanilla and feels like something lewd, especially when it lathers and spreads. The water on my skin, the scent, the steam, my head thrown back, my wet mouth wide … I longed to touch myself, but made myself stop. I held the shower against my buttocks, made them red.

Though I hate office parties, I get here early. I'm warm beneath my dress. My stockings dig a little. (Oh, I've missed you! Phone-sex doesn't work! It's your touch, can't you see that? You left me here alone!) And now, I'm turning. I don't need to think. I sense you there behind me, at the door. The bar is crowded, but I can see you. Your neat black hair, your wide, green eyes. Even from this distance, I can feel your stare. It pushes right into me, tells me what you want.

We don't meet up. We hardly talk. The secret's half the thrill. No one knows about us, and no one ever will. You've kissed me in the closet, in the kitchen, in the hall. You've spanked me after hours, in the silence of your room. But no one ever guesses. And no one guesses now. We circulate, we drink. You pass me, brush my arm. Three times, you touch me in a way that makes me ache. Once, at the bar, you slip your hand across me, just above my buttocks where I will soon be spanked, and the heat from your fingers forces through my flesh and I arch and push against you, full of need. Then, later, when I'm talking to Alissa from Sales, you brush against my arm so I can smell your skin. (That cologne I bought you, the one that smells of spice – it makes me want to lick you, feel your grip.) And at the end of the evening, when the wine has made me flushed, you grab me through my skirt. I gasp, almost moan, but my boss doesn't notice – she's busy talking, like she always is – and you keep on touching me, stroking through my layers, making me so wet my thighs are moist. Then someone calls you over and you move away, and I'm lost without your touch.

At the end of the night, when people start to leave, you're still talking to Matt and Jimmy Sykes. I walk across and join you. Matt's telling a joke. All of us are laughing. I touch your wrist. I think if you don't hurt me within the next few minutes the fire in me will burst. But you don't respond; your eyes stay trained on Matt's. Inside my head, I tell you you're cruel. *Not so*, you reply. *This is how we like it.* And you're right, oh yes, you're right …

At last, you give the cue. You glance at your watch. "It's getting late," you say. "Got jetlag. Better split."

"Me too," I add.

You turn to me, with your wide, certain eyes. Your mouth curls up a little. I've always loved your smile: dry, secretive. I want to bite your lip.

"Shall I get your coat?" you say.

"That's okay. I'll come."

We walk to the coats together. The cloakroom's by the door – an open closet that dips into the wall. You glance across at the drinkers, before pushing me in. I grab the soft layers, moan into their depths; feel you pressing onto me, raising my skirt. My flesh feels so soft. I'm aching, I'm a burn. How I've missed your hands! How I've dreamed of this! I tried, with a ruler, to spank myself like you, but it was merely pain with no relief. I couldn't fake the passion, couldn't fake the need – without you, I'm not *real*. Now I close my eyes. I

96

pray into the air: *Do it, please do it,* afraid you might tease; but you touch my stockings, push your fingers into me, whisper, "Oh, I've missed you," and spank me – once, then twice. My lips part. My breath grows hot. My body jolts with every slap. I push myself against you. I hear you moan and gasp. My legs feel weak beneath me; but you – you feel *strong*. Your spanks become insistent. My buttocks feel sore; but I want harder-harder, so the pleasure takes the pain. And you know it – yes, you know it – because you step right in, and I feel you hard against me as you hit me with your palm. You bite my neck. You gently pull my hair. You touch my mouth and I suck your fingertip. All the time, you're hitting me, swiping at my flesh, so my sex and thighs are wet. And behind us, all those people with their superficial jokes and their stupid power-struggles and their money and their lies, and here are you and I, dirty and alive, stuffed into a corner, getting laid.

But you stop. You pull away. I melt into the coats. "More!" I tell you. "More!" But you stroke down my thigh. I grab a fake-fur and drool into the pelt. I pant, I plead. But you are hard and cruel. You will make me long for you. You will make me wait. And you know that's exactly what I want.

"We'll get a cab," you say. "I know you like cabs."

And yes, you're right. But I tell you this is urgent!

We emerge from the closet. No one seems to notice. But I am a mess, my hair in my face. My stockings rub my thighs, my dress rubs my breasts – each movement makes me sensitised and warm. I whisper in your ear as we walk from the bar, "Aren't you turned on? Say it! You look so cool and calm!" So, in the shadows, you take my hand and place it on your crotch. You're harder than a paperweight. You whisper, "There. You see?" You cup my face and say, "I always, always want you," then you walk me to the cab and help me in.

Behind the driver's screen, you turn me on my side. On the door, there's a bar. I grab this, bite my lip. You reach around my front, lifting up my skirt. You finger me, dip into me, make me sigh and arch. You paddle at my buttocks with the flat of your hand. You play with me. I feel you, stiff against my thigh. You spank me harder, harder. I'm about to come. The heat in me is rising. Pain and pleasure merge. Each bump in the road makes your fingers jolt more deeply. Each turn round a bend makes you fall against my flesh. My eyelids flutter. I whisper, "Yes, oh yes…" And then the cab stops and you abandon me again.

But once we're in my flat, you slam the door shut, and you press me up against the shelf and raise my thigh. And in one move, you're pushing up inside me and your groan is long and beautiful – it makes me lose control. You thrust and I grab you. You spank me, then you bite. I pull you harder into me. I tell you to be harsh. You say that I am perfect. You say that I am yours. You hurt me with such passion that I come.

In the bathroom, I step from my dress. Everything is sticky. Everything is wet. You run the shower, then strip yourself down, and we kiss with our tongues through the steam. You run a finger down my jaw and tell me I am dirty. I laugh into your eyes, and tell you you're worse. And, beneath the spray, you rub me with gel – the stuff you bought in Paris last July. I feel your hands all over me, lathering me up.

We glance down at my buttocks.

They are red.

My New Personal Assistant
by Eva Hore

My boss had employed a new Personal Assistant for me. Her name was Myra. She was efficient and quiet, seemed shy and reserved. We worked together well and I was pleased, as working took my mind off my own personal problems.

A long weekend was coming up. I'd just split with my partner and wasn't interested in a new relationship or even going out. I hated the fact I'd be alone. It had been so much easier having someone in my life even though we'd had our share of problems.

As five o'clock drew near it was just Myra and me left as we made our way to the elevators.

'So what are you up to this weekend?' I asked.

'Nothing,' she said. 'What about you, Vanessa?'

'Same,' I said.

'Why don't you come over to my place? We'll watch videos. You can sleep over,' she said enthusiastically.

Sleep over. I hadn't had a sleep over since I was a little kid. I peered at her and she seemed so eager, so I thought, why not? We could sit around in our pyjamas eating popcorn, watching television, have a little girly night.

'Sure, I'd love to,' I said.

Her eyes lit up, 'Really? Oh we'll have so much fun.'

So that's how it came about that we were lying on her bed in front of the television drinking way too much champagne and eating delicious delicacies, still dressed in our work clothes, minus the shoes.

She popped a movie in and jumped back onto the bed, her skirt riding up high on her thigh. I could see the tops of her stockings and just caught a quick glimpse of her panties. We were laughing about something and didn't notice the credits of the video. Next thing I knew we were watching porn.

'Oops,' she laughed. 'Wonder how that got in there?'

'Hmm, bondage. I've not seen one of these. You into that sort of thing?'

'What?' she spluttered. 'I ... er ... don't know where it came from.'

'It's OK,' I said, 'I have a few at home too.'

'What ... er ...oh. Do you want to watch it?'

'Sure, why not. Never know, I'm might learn something new,' I laughed as I eyed her perky breasts.

As the movie played I found myself getting turned on. I'd never considered being tied up or whipped but the thought of tying up someone else really appealed to me.

'Wonder what it's like being staked out like that,' Myra muttered.

'Why don't I tie you to the bed and you can let me know?' I said, eager for her to comply.

'Yeah, OK,' she said, a little too quickly.

'Take off your stockings,' I said. 'I'll use them.'

As quick as a flash she'd unclipped them. I knew she was a little bit drunk and that I shouldn't take advantage of her, but I couldn't help myself.

'Just open your arms and legs and spread both wide,' I said.

She giggled as I tied her securely to the bed.

I looked over my shoulder at the video and saw a guy munching down on this woman's pussy and I thought, why not?

Pulling aside her panties, I looked hungrily at her pussy.

'Hey, what are you doing?' she said.

'Just following what they're doing on the video. Come on, it will be fun to experiment a little, won't it?'

'Oh, OK,' she said in a quiet voice.

I lay between her outstretched legs, her pussy visible to me. I'd never gone down on a woman before and found myself excited at the prospect. Her pussy lips protruded nicely as I pulled her panties across, causing them to bulge forward. I could just see her inner lips poking out of her slit and, with the curiosity of a child, I tentatively stretched my tongue forward, to have my first lick, my first taste.

I felt her pull back and she moaned, 'Oh!'

I wasn't sure if she liked it or not so I did it again.

'Oh, yeah,' she moaned.

Encouraged, I licked harder, my tongue roaming around as my fingers pulled her outer lips apart.

'Oh, yeah, that feels good,' she breathed sexily, all the girlishness now gone.

Her scent wafted up to me and I nuzzled in further, licking in between her folds as my fingers began to explore inside her.

'Oh, man,' I breathed. 'You're so wet. This is turning you on, is it?' I chuckled.

'You bet, bitch,' she hissed at me.

Whoa, I thought. Where did that come from?

'Lick me. Lick me hard, you fucker,' she swore. 'Tear my shirt off and suck my tits.'

Not wanting to come across too innocent, after all I was her boss, I tore her shirt apart, buttons flying everywhere and exposed her heaving breasts.

'Suck them,' she demanded.

Knowing she was at my mercy, I hesitated, wanting her to beg. I ran my hands over the swell of her breasts before inching my fingers inside her bra and giving each nipple a tweak.

'Suck them,' she demanded, wriggling desperately.

She had on one of those bras that opened at the front and as I unclipped them her breasts literally popped forward, her nipples hard and rigid.

'Suck them hard,' she whispered throatily. 'Suck them fucking hard.'

Lowering my head I took a nipple into my mouth, rolled it around my tongue, my saliva slipping all over it, while I crushed the other.

'Oh, God, yeah,' she breathed. 'Suck it in, baby.'

Not wanting her to call all the shots I pulled back.

'Hey,' she complained. 'Get back here.'

I looked down at her, practically naked, and decided I'd make her wait. Wanting to come across as the dom I left her there while I looked for things to heighten this experience like I'd seen on many of my own videos.

'Untie me,' she demanded just as I spied a pair of scissors on her dresser.

Lifting her skirt to her waist, I put the outside blade against her skin just above her slit. She sucked in her breath not daring now to speak. I eyed her mischievously, smirking while she licked her lips, wondering if I'd harm her.

In one quick movement I slashed her panties from her, exposing her completely. Now her pussy and her tits were mine for the taking.

'Please,' she begged, tugging at the restraints, 'make love to me.'

I threw myself between her open thighs, my tongue lapping at her. I wiggled between her cheeks trying to lick her hole and then slathered her with saliva and made my way up over her slit and under her hood, where her clit was nestling as though waiting for me.

'Oh yeah baby. Ohhh, yeah. Tickle it, rub your tongue up against it, yeah like that. Now with your finger … oh yeah …that's it … don't stop … ohhh … ohhhh … don't stop … I'm coming … coming … ahhh.'

With my finger rubbing like mad I watched as her juices poured out of her. Fascinated, I lapped them up. Her scent intoxicated me and I went wild, nuzzling into her cunt, grabbing her breasts, squeezing them, pinching the nipples while I smothered myself in her pussy.

'Oh that's so great ….bring your pussy up here … I want to taste you too … come on … please, turn yourself around.'

Before I assumed the 69 position over her I stripped out of my stockings and panties, positioning my cleanly waxed pussy just inches from her mouth.

'Stop teasing me,' she moaned. 'Let me taste you.'

Lowering my pussy over her waiting mouth, I could feel her breath on me, tantalizing my skin, before her tongue touched me, sending a fire searing through me, making me feel more alive than I have in my whole life.

This little mouse was now a tiger. She lifted her head into my pussy, licking furiously, her tongue locating my clit as she flickered it over me like a madwoman. As she buried herself into me I untied her legs, grabbing at the stocking, tearing them in my haste to free her.

I turned myself around and untied her arms while her legs wrapped around my waist. She flew at me, grabbing me, kissing me, her scent and mine mingling together as our lips and mouths met.

'Oh fuck,' I moaned, never having felt anything so good.

'You taste great,' she breathed as her tongue trailed down my neck and into the cleavage of my bra.

'Take off the rest of your clothes,' she demanded.

In a flash I was naked and from under the bed she produced a switch. This little mouse had played this game before.

'You were very naughty,' she said, grabbing at my breasts. 'Very naughty not to untie me earlier. Now you will have to be punished.'

I couldn't wait. The thought of that switch whipping me was driving me insane. I wanted nothing more and eagerly waited for her instructions.

She jumped from the bed, demanding I kneel on the floor and rest my torso over the bed. She stood behind me and I heard the switch whistle through the air before a thousand tiny fingers ignited my skin.

On and on she lashed, my back, arms and then lower to my cheeks and thighs. I've never felt anything so amazing in my life.

My pussy throbbed as the welts rose. She whipped me

again and again while I buried my moans in her pillow. Then she turned the switch around, traced a pattern on my back, then lower down the crack of my arse. I tensed as she played around my puckered hole.

'You're enjoying this, aren't you?' she demanded.

I said nothing, unsure of whether or not I should speak.

She pushed my thighs apart and her hand went underneath cupping my pussy.

'Oh, you love it alright,' she laughed. 'You're so wet it's dripping down my fingers.'

'No I don't,' I whimpered.

'Don't lie to me,' she commanded, as the handle plunged straight into me.

'Oh yes,' I whispered as she fucked me with it. 'Oh yes.'

'You horny little bitch,' she said. 'Roll over onto the bed. Get up there and spread those legs.'

I did as she said. Lying there with my legs splayed open for her to see every inch of me.

The porno movie was still going on in the background and I snuck a look over at it, saw three women rolling around on a bed together, before a slap on the thigh reminded me it was her I was suppose to be focused on.

Then she was slapping at my pussy, the switch tantalizing me, hot fingers igniting my passion further until my clit swelled, the blood pooling there as my passion increased.

'Masturbate,' she demanded.

I didn't need to be asked twice, I was itching to come.

'Oh, yeah, she said.

I wanted nothing more than some sexual release and eagerly rubbed myself as she watched. She pushed the handle of the switch into my pussy and began to fuck me with it while I orgasmed around it.

She fell on me bringing me to a height I'd never thought possible and later we lay together, our fingers stroking and exploring, eager to touch every inch of each other's bodies.

Thank God for long weekends and her endless supply of videos. We spent all three days and nights enjoying each other and now sometimes when we're feeling randy at work we sneak off into the storeroom to relieve each other.

I can with absolute certainty say that my Personal Assistant knows exactly what my needs and desires are.

Mistress Satina's Slutmaid Academy
by Alexia Falkendown

Weekends are always interesting when I have a full class of six trainees attending my Satina's Select Slutmaid Academy at my elegant Regency residence in Brighton's Royal Pavilion Square. They arrive from London on Friday afternoon and Adelaide, my collared submissive partner and Academy Supervisor, soon has them sissydressed and ready for my inspection when I make my first entrance at Evening Assembly in my bijou ballroom.

I insist that trainee Slutmaids commence their scheduled weekends of intensive disciplined training by submitting to Adelaide's strict but enjoyable feminization routine; a sensual bubble bath followed by body depilation and creaming, (I abominate hairy Slutmaids), a manicure and a facial. Only then are they ready to be tightly laced up into their form-shaping satin corset, and step into their custom-made Slutmaid's uniform. Adelaide supervises each postulant Slutmaid as she masters the feminine art of facial make-up and checks her dress prior to my inspection. Woe betide Slutmaid (and Adelaide), if I am displeased with their appearance.

I make my entrance on the dot of 8 o'clock and six tightly corseted and newly curvaceous Slutmaids, feeling deliciously feminine in their satin and heels, make a low curtsy and chorus a greeting, "Good Evening Mistress Satina!" Adelaide has them charmingly dressed in their black satin ruffle maid uniforms with short flouncy skirts that show off frilly white petticoats and allow a tantalizing glimpse of black satin-and-lace 'slut-hole' knickers. Their fetching sissy ensemble is completed by sheer black, lace-topped seamed stockings held tautly against their creamed and smoothed thighs by their corset suspenders.

I like to compliment each Slutmaid on her turnout and course progress. Sometimes, however, I must discipline a Sissyslut for wayward behaviour the previous weekend and give her solemn notice to present herself for a bare bottom spanking the following evening.

For serious misdemeanors I give a naughty Slutmaid 24 hours warning before caning her in front of her assembled sissymates at my weekly Saturday evening 'Punishment Parade'. The wait heightens her apprehension, allowing her to anticipate the impending pain and the humiliation of baring her bottom in submission before all.

I am a strict disciplinarian, but I am also a loving Mistress! I reward a novice Slutmaid who has been diligent and amenable in her studies the previous weekend with a sensual lovestrapping on Friday evening. Stripped to a figure-hugging white corset that enhances and shapes her sissified body and displays the beauty of her rounded bottom, I have Adelaide bend her over and tether her to my punishment block in the ballroom. After lowering her knickers, I give her squirming butt 100 teasing lashes with my velvet-suede flogger, occasionally flicking the jewels dangling enticingly between her legs or pausing to caress her pussycock to tumescent arousal. My sensual coordination of caress and sting brings her writhing body to a euphoric pitch that can only be satiated by Mistress Satina's gloved hand stroking that heated slutcock to its ecstatic peak of spurting slutcum.

There would be no slutcock ecstasies handed out by me this Friday, however. But there would be a severe caning for a tearful Slutmaid on Saturday.

Clumsily breaking one of my precious Royal Worcester teacups the previous weekend while pouring my Earl Grey at Sunday afternoon tea in the garden, Slutmaid Candy had stained my favourite satin blouse. Although she had telephoned from London during the week to inform Adelaide that she had purchased a complete replacement bone china tea service at Harrods and had spent £160 on a pleasing new blouse at a Knightsbridge designer boutique, such waywardness cannot go unpunished!

I left Candy until last in my inspection. She knew her inevitable fate and knelt at my feet.

"I am a very clumsy Slutmaid, Mistress! Please punish me!"

"I shall whip you tomorrow evening!" I said curtly.

A titillating thought struck me. "Since Adelaide is your supervisor, she is equally culpable."

I smiled frostily. "I shall cane her too!"

Adelaide's sharp intake of breath and the excited murmur of salacious anticipation from the assembled Slutmaids were music to my ears as I swept haughtily from the room.

The prospect of bending Slutmaid Candy and Adelaide over the punishment block and caning their bared bottoms to an erotically arousing picture of sunset red put me in a festive mood. The rounded cheeks of a bared bottom, framed by corset, suspenders, seamed stockings and high heels, create a visually beautiful, sensually arousing and emotionally alluring picture. My darling Adelaide looks her most adorable, vulnerable and beautiful when she willingly positions herself for punishment. I love the sweet symmetry of her upended plump bottom, quivering with loving and slightly fearful anticipation of the pain to come. It bounces provocatively to each stinging kiss from my cane.

Having often been caned myself by Pandora, my first sapphic lover and Domina lifestyle mentor, many years ago, I appreciate the dread thrill of anticipation such a humiliatingly helpless yet provocative stance engenders in the bosom of both the chastised and her chastiser. It is an addictive and emotionally charged bond between every Domina and her submissive.

Properly orchestrated and enacted at a measured pace with

flickering candles, euphoric incense and throbbing music to enhance the ritualistic drama of the scene, a caning becomes a sacred communion; a mystic union of unspoken bliss between loving Mistress and her whipped submissive. It is an inspirational and memorably arousing experience too, for those onlookers who are fortunate to participate as silent witnesses. Their presence heightens the ritualistic tension.

I knew my caning of Candy and Adelaide would lead to a most satisfactory climax for us. There would be a mutual explosion of sensual desire and orgasmic surrender to the imperious demands of my aroused body when I took them both to my boudoir for my 'Afterglow' partyplay of tongue, pussycock and dildo.

When Adelaide finished her Saturday evening deportment lesson, she dismissed the class, sending them to their rooms to prepare themselves for the 'Punishment Parade' in which her own bouncy bottom was to feature in such delightful prominence alongside Candy's.

Before sending her off to prepare for her appointment with pain, I gave Adelaide precise instructions on the dramatic setting I required for our punishment scene when I entered the ballroom: lighted candles in the antique corner candelabras, jasmine incense slowly curling from a brazier on the Chinese lacquer sideboard and, most importantly, the positioning of the Victorian whipping block which serves as our 'altar' to Nemesis, Goddess of Punishment. I required Ravel's Boléro to be throbbing in the background. It builds to an arousing crescendo and intensity; the perfect slow beat for my purpose. I would time my caning strokes to Ravel's hypnotic beat.

Adelaide's lovely face turned a lighter shade of pale beneath her make-up at my instructions. Her anal flower was doubtlessly twitching in thrilled but fearful anticipation of the searing pain I intended to inflict upon her delectable derrière; pain that she knew would prelude a night of mutual lust and orgasmic ecstasy when I took her proffered body in 'Afterglow' partyplay.

She was waiting in my boudoir when I arrived to dress for

the evening's activities after enjoying my evening champagne cocktail in the drawing room. She had put up her long auburn tresses into a tight chignon at the back of her head to display the hammered gold torque with which I had collared her as my Submissive Bride. She had provocatively 'undressed' for the occasion. She was sans knickers beneath her crimson sateen corset that supported the ripe fullness of her exposed breasts with the large brown aureoles I so loved to nibble. It framed the smooth softness of her Venus mound that I so loved to tongue. The matching sheer stockings and lace-up high-heeled boots completed her come-hither ensemble.

Disrobing me of my pencil skirt, satin blouse and Agent Provocateur bra, she helped me into the black sateen corset I wear for flagellatory exercise, fastening its six suspenders to my black stockings. My corset fits like the skin of a cobra, molding itself to the contours of my well kept body; emphasizing my trim waist, the swell of my rounded hips and the curve of my firm buttocks. It erotically displays my 'Brazilian', emphasizes the 'cameltoe' of my ever hungry lovelips and supports my bared breasts, giving them proud prominence while leaving them free to swing as I wield my cane.

My sensual arousal did not pass unnoticed by Adelaide as she ran her hand lasciviously over my breasts and down the smooth curves of my body to my cunt, her eyes fixed longingly on my thrusting tits. Sensing her excitement, my nipples stiffened to her passing touch. I cupped a breast and guided her wanton lips to its erect succulence.

"Suck me, my sweet slave!"

She smiled and began to suck greedily. I felt a flowing moistness that needed a mouth to assuage the hidden turmoil building in the pit of my uterus. I pressed her down and crushed her head to my cunt.

"Tongue me, sweet slave! Worship your Mistress before she whips you to Elysium and back!"

Adelaide has a serpentine tongue! My now engorged clit responded to her oscular ministrations in very short time and her agile tonguing quickly brought me to a quivering peak, bringing a flooding cumsquirt to her adoring lips that had her gasping as she lapped my joyjuices.

It was time for Mistress to retake control before this party got out of hand!

"Enough of your salacious dallying, Slave! Get your plump 'partygoods' down to the ballroom and prepare to entertain me!"

They stood in silent apprehension when I entered the ballroom with my cane. Adelaide had stripped Slutmaid Candy of her satin and lace and she was sans knickers in appropriately virginal white sateen corset, stockings and heels. This was her first ever caning and I could see she was distinctly nervous at being Mistress Satina's whipping 'bride', having doubtless heard of my flagellatory prowess and predilections from Adelaide.

I always place my 'Altar to Nemesis' punishment block before a full-length wall mirror to afford me and those I punish the additional pleasure, or agony, of watching their humiliation. The altar looks like a padded gym horse with six stout mahogany legs with parallel crossbars each side. Buckled leather straps attached to each leg provide secure restraints to shackle miscreants positioned for punishment.

I undid the buckles, checked the height of the padded top against the girls' waists with a professional eye and stood back. Adelaide knew the drill and moved forward to settle herself in the required caning position, but Candy needed to be led through the punishment procedure.

"Bend over the altar and settle your stomach comfortably on the padding. Part your legs so I can tether you and, more importantly, see your jewels dangling between your legs."

Candy opened her legs to be shackled. She gasped, overcome by the tension as she felt the cold leather padding against her belly and slutcock and reached over to grip the horizontal bar. If she had not been wearing fetish spike heels she would have been on tiptoe."

I stood back to inspect their bottoms now bared before me,

so erotically framed by corsets, suspenders, stockings and heels.

"Settle onto the punishment altar and arch your back to 'present' your bottom to Nemesis!"

Adelaide arched obediently and 'presented', enabling me to see the sweet pink pucker of her tight little fuckbutton. Below it peeked the swollen lovelips that would later welcome my thrusting dildo and questing tongue at our 'Afterglow' partyplay. They were enticingly open and moistly glistening in the flickering candlelight; souvenir of our earlier boudoir play.

"Raise your head, square your shoulders and straighten your arms! Your breasts must not be resting on the altar! "

Adelaide raised her head as instructed, letting her her rounded globes dangle in pendulous freedom, but Candy had little to dangle! She gasped again at the mounting tension and a nervous tremor coursed down her stockinged thigh.

I took my stance, rubbed the long rattan speculatively along the tender 'sweet spot' on the two bottoms posed before me.

"Prepare for punishment!"

They raised their pretty cheeks higher. Candy's heavy jewels swayed with her movement. I flexed my cane, feeling its whippy springiness and enjoying the sound it made as it whisked through the air. I paused, raised the cane over my head, the rod parallel to the ground, poised as if parrying a sabre thrust to the head. Fearful eyes met mine in the mirror's reflection. The music surged.

Crack! Crack!

I whipped the rattan down in a circular motion in quick cuts that cracked like pistol shots across each bottom. Scorching angry red lines of pain traced across the tender underside of Adelaide's sweetcheeks and Candy's more androgynous buttocks; two perfectly executed examples of the infamous 'Coup de Cavalerie', perfected by La Fouetteuse, Paris's most illustrious Dominatrix.

Adelaide screamed as a burning fire shot through her body. She bucked in involuntary reaction to the pain, grinding her cunt against the punishment altar. Candy yelled and shot bolt upright, rubbing feverishly at her slutcheeks.

"Get back down or I shall give you an added stroke every time you move!"

She returned hastily to her 'present' position, snorting with pain.

I struck twice more at the rapidly reddening bottoms, each 'Cavalry Cut' landing a cane's width higher than the previous one. Two bottoms now quivered before my gaze from the fire of the three cuts which had scored burning lines across the tender lower curve of their cheeks. Adelaide was crying and Candy sweating, quivers coursing down her leg as she writhed, ineffectively attempting to clench her slutcheeks against the cuts.

I changed my stance to draw the cane back parallel to the three red stripes seared across the lower curves of their ravaged cheeks. My 'wrist-flick' technique, which will one day bring me accolades in those esoteric Domina circles where caning technique is discussed, brought the rod sharply back and forward to strike in whipping flashes that bent the rod in its speed of delivery, etching brilliant red weals of pain across the centre of each twitching bottom. In strictly measured time to Ravel's throbbing beat, I delivered two final flicking parallel strokes to each with cold, cruel accuracy.

It was over! I lowered the cane and moved forward to inspect my artistry and feel the heat of the raised welts with my hand. It was a perfect caning! It left a set of six parallel stripes across their bottom cheeks in a visually pleasing four inch bandwidth of burning crimson. They would be turning to a purple hue by the time I took them to my boudoir later that evening for our 'Afterglow' partyplay.

"You may rise!"

My two gifts to the Goddess Nemesis stood up from the punishment altar, tenderly exploring the stinging welts on their bottoms. Streaky lines of mascara marked the passage of tears down their faces.

I released them from their restraints and like a mother who comforts her children after scolding them, took them into my arms and held them tight as they began to sob in relief at the end of their ordeal.

Behind us, five Slutmaids stood hypnotized in fascinated silence. The scene had been arousing, too arousing for some! They had their slutcocks out of their satin knickers and were stroking each other feverishly. I would cane them in due course for such 'slutruttish' behaviour in my presence.

The ritual had brought me to my customary wetness of arousal. My throbbing cunt was now aching for the orgasmic release that I always need after such a 'Domina High' and power-surge engendered by a caning ritual upon the willing body of a submissive lover or Slutmaid. No caning is complete without that release and I knew that both Adelaide and Candy would soon be panting for my very personal attention! In confirmation, I felt the warm throb of Slutmaid Candy's tumescent slutcock rub against my thigh. It was high time for 'Afterglow' partyplay! I would to take her now to my boudoir for Adelaide to milk that slutcock to its explosive release while I introduced Candy's lovebutton to the pleasure of my thrusting dildo.

A sudden question crossed my mind. "Have you been ever been buttfucked?"

Candy looked down demurely and blushed. "No! Will it hurt?"

I smiled at her innocence and kissed her lightly. "Not with Mistress! She will be especially tender with her sore-bottomed slutvirgin!"

Candy knelt to my cunt and nuzzled at my moist lovelips.

"Take me darling Mistress! Take the rest of my slutbody and deflower me! I surrender myself to your will!"

A questing tongue flicked tentatively at my hooded pearl.

My intended 'Afterglow' had suddenly taken on an unexpected new dimension.

We were wasting good playtime! I led the two sore bottoms upstairs to my candlelit boudoir.

Ensconced upon the satin expanse of my boudoir Ottoman we

made an interesting threesome. Adelaide and I had discarded our corsets, stockings and heels which lay in a jumbled heap on the silk carpet. Candy was kneeling to suck at Adelaide's exposed pussy, tonguefucking her pink sweetness while frigging her aroused clit. Adelaide had her head between Candy's knees and was fondling and sucking her dangling jewels and stroking that slutcock to heated erection. I stood behind Candy contemplating her striped slutcheeks and the inviting fuckbutton that was displayed so enticingly to the eight inch long dildo strapped to my thighs, its hidden alter-dildo gripped moistly tight within me by my powerful vaginal muscles.

Taking some lube, I applied it tenderly to Candy's pink button. A responsive quiver racked her body and her virgin bud involuntarily opened in welcome. She squirmed to allow my probing finger to breach her virginal hole and delve deeper inside her. The slippery sucking of the Slutmaid's anal muscles on my finger brought an anticipatory quiver of excitement to my cunt.

I caressed the tortured heat of Candy's delectable slutcheeks for a moment, savouring the vision of my hot stripes now glowing upon her smooth twitching globes.

"Today, I gave you bottom pain!" I pressed my dildo's knob to her exposed anal flower. "Now, I give you bottom pleasure!"

I thrust my shaft to pierce Candy's weak defences. Her lubed button offered just token resistance, submitting gratefully to a new and thrilling sensation as I pressed home. I slid slowly, inexorably, inch by inch, into her sweet sluthole's welcoming grip, forcing my stiff strength ever deeper into her enveloping slippery tightness. She moaned contentedly, luxuriating in the feeling of fullness within her engendered by my rigid weapon. She squirmed to accommodate the rampant beast, working her anal muscles to grip and massage it on its oiled journey, while Adelaide stroked her pulsing slutcock and fondled her warm plums. Finally I felt my lovelips slapping against the heat of her bruised slutcheeks. I had taken Candy's slutvirginity.

I took my tawse and began to whip my Slutmaid's splayed slutcheeks in time to my thrusting onslaught, cracking down left and right with overhand and backhand strokes to her responsive arse, stinging each already reddened cheek to an even deeper blush with the leather's spanking kisses. Candy moaned in ecstasy, squirming excitedly to the stinging goad, her skewered slutbuns writhing to the rhythmic movement of my slapping leather and pumping thrust, her now hard slutcock facefucking Adelaide's slurping mouth.

I started Candy at a slow trot, sliding into the tight silken embrace of her welcoming fuckbutton, then retreating until only the dildo's mushroom head was held in her anal grip. I quickened my thrusts, slapping her haunches, spurring her on to a canter. Finally I flashed my tawse from one crimson cheek to the other, goading her into the frenzy of a galloping buttfuck.

"Aaah-ugh! Aaah-ugh! Aaah-ugh!"

Candy's panting frenzy and gasping grunts of pleasure matched the thrusting rhythm of my dildo as I pumped deep into her gut while Adelaide deepthroated her hot slutcock.

She broke away for a moment from cunnysucking Adelaide.

"Fuck me! Suck me! Ride me! Break me to your bridle!"

We were each at full stretch now; my nostrils flaring in frenzied lust, as I spurred my slutmount to the ecstasy of her first thrilling bottomfuck while Adelaide bucked and writhed to Candy's frenzied tonguing.

"Fuck my pinkie arsehole, Mistress! Suck my juicy lollycock, Adelaide! Roast me!"

We responded to her urgings. I fucked! Adelaide sucked!

I dropped the tawse and dug my talons into Candy's writhing hips, thrusting ever faster and deeper in a wild fury, punching my cuntcock to the hilt. Adelaide slurped at the slippery hardness of Candy's pumping slutcock. Candy felt me jerk to my peaking frenzy … my heated breath upon her neck … my panting grunts … my triumphant cry … and then my hot, spurting deluge of joycum over her buttocks and Adelaide's upturned face as I melted in the squirting joy of an explosive orgasm. It was the signal for Candy to climax, spurting her cream of orgasmic joy in hot globules of slutcum over Adelaide's face.

While my fuckbuddies lay totally spent, I tottered over to the wardrobe and exchanged my used dildo for Adelaide's special favourite and returned to stimulate them both to new life. The night was young and so was I!

Adelaide parted her legs, spreading wide her pink labia to offer her clitoral pearl to me.

"Come, my darling Mistress! You need your Collarbaby after such an energetic night! Cum and collect your favourite pussyprize!"

She raised her pelvis. "Here it is, waiting for you to ride me. Bitch me! Bitch your Collarslut! Fuck me, darling! Remind me why I worship you so!"

I climbed onto her, sliding my cuntcock smoothly into her moistly welcoming hole. I pressed my lips to her open mouth, smothering her dirty talk, my tongue entwining with hers in serpentine embrace. I began to pump, thrusting our dildo deep, its thumping rhythm sending ripples of energy to my own insatiable lovehole. Adelaide squeezed her cunt muscles, gripping my weapon and massaging it with her juices as I thrust, withdrew and thrust again.

"Oh my darling Mistress! Fuck me to oblivion! Fuck your little slaveslut!"

She squirmed lasciviously beneath me, kneading my tits, twisting at my hard nipples, urging me on to yet another climax.

I rode my loveslave with hard, thumping frenzy now, the alter-dildo polishing my pearl to bring me to the high peak I so desperately needed after our sensual whipping scene.

I felt a new, more powerful climax rising as Adelaide spurred me on with her guttermouthing.

"Fuck me, you dominating bitch! Ravish me! Cock-whip me to Elysium, you heavenly cunt-fucker. Tear my vagina!

Harder! Harder!"

I tipped over the precipice in an explosive flash of orgasmic energy. I stopped her lips in passionate kiss; sucking, tonguing, biting, clawing at her heaving breasts as the joy coursed through me for the third time. It transmitted its energy to Adelaide pinioned beneath me. She quivered, shuddered and entwined her legs around me in a vice-like grip, joining me in her own flooding orgasm. Our lovejuices mingled in pulsing union.

I rose and discarded my dripping strap-on. It was time for us to rouse our rosy-cheeked Candy Slutbitch resting languidly beside us and educate her in the art of pearl diving.

Bodyguard
by Laurel Aspen

'Get out of my way dammit, do you have any idea who I am?'

Blonde – well, from an expensive bottle at least – and tempestuous the struggling spitfire's shrieks of protest shattered the expensive ambience of the exclusive *prêt a porter* emporium.

'Yes ma'am, I do, you're Columbia Walker, but I'm afraid it makes no difference.' The Paul Smith be-suited floorwalker remained impressively calm under verbal fire.

'Of course it makes a goddamn difference. I'm not an ordinary shopper, not one of the little people, the usual rules don't apply; I was simply taking the items to try on in a more secluded changing area.'

'That's not what our cameras show ma'am.'

'What cameras? I face cameras when I'm paid to and at no other time.'

'Our in-store CCTV security screens clearly revealed you heading for the door with no intention of paying for those goods…'

'It's customary for stars to be loaned items to wear to wear at the Oscars, you fool.'

'Maybe, but it ain't our custom and I'm going to have to call the police.'

'Hey, what's goin' on?' A second man intervened.

'Jon, thank goodness; tell this moron here to let me go immediately.'

'What's the problem, Ms Walker?'

'Problem? It's not a problem, it's an outrage; this oaf is accusing me of shoplifting!'

'OK buddy what's the story, hey you're…'

'I don't believe it, Jon.'

'Frank!'

'Jeez what a place to meet.'

'Long time, man.'

'And some.'

'When you two are through with old home week perhaps someone might like to explain how come you're so obviously acquainted.' The woman's sarcasm was biting.

'Both ex-airborne, Ms Walker,' explained Jon.

'Served in the Gulf together,' agreed Frank heartily, 'plus a few other places Uncle Sam'd rather we didn't discuss. Hell this guy saved me from losing an arm one time.'

'Hey it wasn't that dramatic buddy,' responded Jon with characteristic modesty, 'look, how 'bout we go somewhere and sort this out?'

'I shouldn't, but, well I guess if you're working for Ms Walker…'

'He's my personal security operative,' spat the otherwise attractive young woman angrily, 'and had he been paying attention this might never…'

'Ahem, if you'd like to go into that office there,' suggested Frank diplomatically.

Columbia flounced angrily across the floor and the two men followed, talking quietly. 'Sheesh, she always seemed real nice in her films, when'd she turn into ball breaking bitch of the decade?' queried Frank.

'About six months back,' replied Jon, still smarting at his boss's public put down.

'How long you worked for her man?'

'I guess around 18 months, started off a good gig, like you say she use to come on pretty much as she appeared in the movies,' said Jon.

'But?'

'Two Hollywood blockbusters in succession; megabucks followed by a hoard of fawning sycophants. Miss Superstar here started to believe the studio publicity about her was the real deal,' sighed Jon wearily.

'Kinda "Day of the Locust" for the new millennium' suggested Frank.

'Very perceptive as ever my friend,' Jon replied. 'Yeah Columbia began comin' on like a spoilt child an' when the next movie turned out to be a turkey she threw the longest hissy fit LA's every seen.'

'Then publicity like this she don't need.' averred Frank.

'Meaning?' Jon smiled, as if he could already guess the answer.

'Meanin' firstly that I owe you one for bailing me out when that Chinook went down...'

'And?'

'This job sucks man, it was meant to be a temp thing but I've been here nine month, this lousy shoppin' mall's suckin' the life outta me,' Frank sounded tired.

'What do you need?'

'Always the sharp one,' Frank nodded approvingly, 'I'll cut straight to the chase. I ain't greedy man. Twenty grand buys me a share in pal's scuba diving school off Key West. Sort me out in cash and you an' Shirley Temple can hit the exit with the security video tape long before management starts asking questions.'

'Frank, you're a star but I'm gonna haggle with you,' began Jon. 'No,' he raised a hand to still his erstwhile buddy's objection. 'Cheap at twice the price, I won't settle for a dollar less than $40,000, little Ms Moneybags won't even notice it, I've seen her spend that much on shoes.'

'Well thank god you got finally got your sloppy act together at the 11th hour.' Columbia was darting angrily around her Laurel Canyon A frame, high heels clattering on the beech parquet, a tight pencil skirt forcing her to take short rapid steps.

Jon leant his six-foot frame against the doorjamb and did

some breathing exercises to slow his rising heart beat and stay calm. Although neither as tall nor as broad as his erstwhile comrade in arms, the now Florida-bound store detective, Jon Bradley, corn-fed American boy, was every inch a former soldier. Underneath the neat denim shirt and chinos he packed some serious power. Not gym-pumped steroid bulges but long sinewy muscles, twelve stone of strength and stamina matched by a mind which had put him a whole different ball park from the average grunt. A former bodyguard to Jack Nicholson and Angelica Houston, Jon was usually professionally geared to tactfully avoid conflict, but right now he'd had enough.

'Shut up!' He raised his voice only slightly but the icy tone was enough to momentarily halt Columbia's self-regarding rambles.

'First of all you deliberately gave me the slip like some silly little kid playing truant.'

'Hey I…' Columbia's indignant interjection was cut off with a single withering look.

'Second I do not get off on having my professionalism publicly undermined. Grow up girl, start being accountable for your own actions; you got yourself into that situation not me.'

Columbia gasped; an uncomfortable jolt of truth gnawed at her stomach; prudently, if wholly uncharacteristically, for once she didn't interrupt.

'Thirdly you have gone from a smart, sassy indy movie star to winner of the Joan Crawford award for solipsism; head so far up your too-often kissed ass you've no longer any perspective on the outside world or consideration for us mere mortals who inhabit it.'

'You can't talk to me like that,' yelled Columbia relocating her inner shrew and finally finding her shrill voice, 'you're fired.'

'Lady, I quit,' Jon's voice was dangerously quiet, 'but before I go I'm gonna try and stop the rot, do you a favour and above all get me some recompense for the last six months of hell.'

'What do you mean? Get away, don't touch me.' The look

of determination on Jon's face had Columbia scared. Silently he strode towards her and grabbed her wrist.

'No,' she screamed pathetically holding up her hands, 'don't damage my face.'

'Oh you don't have to worry 'bout that pretty face,' Jon said grimly. 'If you'd taken the trouble to understand me as well as I do you, you'd know I never beat up on a woman in my life. I was raised by a single mom and taught respect. Pity your '60s liberal hippy parents didn't do the same. 'However,' he added, plonking himself onto an uncomfortably modern and angular chair and pulling her over his lap, 'I intend to make a small exception.'

'Let me go!' Columbia screeched in horror as his intention suddenly became plain.

'Who's gonna make me?' asked Jon, savouring the humour of his erstwhile employer's situation, 'the bodyguard?'

'What the hell do you think you're doing?' whined the supine star, scarily certain she already knew.

'I know exactly what I'm at,' growled Jon, lifting her slender frame effortlessly from the floor and pinning her face down, struggling and kicking, over his knee.

'You wouldn't,' her voice tried for a coquettish, pleading tone, 'dare spank me?'

'Oh yes I would,' Jon confirmed happily, 'this spoilt butt is overdue for a thorough tanning, a whole galaxy of waiters, maids, directors, agents, fellow actors and fans deserve to witness this comeuppance, but sadly only I have the privilege.'

'Get off, this is assault, I'll report you, I'll sue,' Columbia was frantic; she'd never yet encountered a man she couldn't wheedle her way around.

'Like I care, like anyone will believe you,' he laughed, 'and anyway the National Enquirer will have a field day. I can see the headline now: "Film Star gets her ass whipped." Great chance to test the theory that any publicity is good publicity.'

'No!' yelled Columbia despairingly, legs flailing, head down and bum uppermost as Jon wrestled her tight skirt up around her still enviably trim 24 inch, 24 year old waist.

123

'Legs to beat the band,' mused the ex-soldier as he skilfully dodged those lethal flailing stiletto heels. Her perfect peach of a carefully dieted, personally trained bum was currently sheathed in sheer grey tights and ivory coloured panties. Which, it transpired as Jon's hand began the first of many impacts, loudly and firmly across her rippling moons, held her buttocks perfectly in position but offered no protection at all.

Had this been one of the foreplay spankings he'd occasionally dispensed to lovers, Jon would have began slowly, gradually building up the tempo and velocity of contact to match his partner's arousal and allowing lengthy interludes for soothing caresses and intimate stroking. This however was a punishment spanking, the release of months of tension, retribution for a thousand slights and he'd every intention that the little cow would feel it from the start and still smart painfully tomorrow.

Fifty or more ringing slaps set the tone, turned her skin from lightly tanned to blushing pink; sent a fierce, fiery stinging pain flaring across every inch of her tormented hindquarters. In response to which Columbia shouted, protested, cried, writhed and generally disported herself without out an ounce of dignity.

Jon paused for breath and, thinking his anger abated and her penance at an end, Columbia gave a shuddering sigh of premature relief, which abruptly became a keening moan as her tights and knickers were pulled rudely to her knees.

Oh woe, the ultimate embarrassment, Hollywood's hottest young female star spanked humiliatingly bare across the knees of the help. OK, pretty hunky help, it was true. Hey, where did that thought come from? Grasshopper brain. How could Columbia possibly be thinking about sex at this awful moment? But she'd be lying if she didn't admit that looks had been a factor in Jon's employment.

Or that she'd sometimes entertained fantasises of his physique, all the better to dismiss the memory of studio-promoted public dates with yet another *ersatz* tough guy actor. But this situation involved an embarrassing lack of control she'd hardly bargained for. Down came his hand, again and again, jerking her back to a sore reality and leaving imprints of pale fire on the increasingly scarlet hued skin of her scalded nether cheeks

'Ow, ow, ow!' It stung, it was hot, it hurt and she really couldn't take any more. Tears welled up, washing her makeup in rivulets down her cheeks as Columbia gave loud vent to her contrite and confused feelings.

Jon's wasn't intrinsically unkind, he'd nothing more to prove, and indeed he seriously considered concluding the chastisement there and then. Instead he decided to be cruel to be kind. Somewhere inside he still held some affection for Columbia, maybe a salutary lesson might make her regain her equilibrium, undergo a damascene personality change, cure a movie brat.

In pursuit of which laudable blind faith he pulled the belt from his trousers, doubled it and wop, wop, wop, concluded her torment with a dozen harsh, searing strokes across Columbia's tenderised haunches, leaving livid parallel weals from the crest of her buttocks to the tops of her thighs.

The sobbing prima donna was now beyond struggle, beyond pain, existing !in a blazing hell of draconian discipline, which would ensure she ate standing up next day and slept on her stomach, if at all. Finally satisfied his self-appointed task was complete, Jon tumbled the chastened thespian weeping and dishevelled to the floor, reacquainted the broad strip of leather with his belt loops and strode from the room. Two hours later – as a tear streaked and shocked Columbia still knelt by the chair massaging her ravaged rear – he was on a flight to Hawaii.

More than a year later, completely out of the blue, Jon retrieved her letter in his mailbox. Off the beaten tack but not completely isolated, the modern wonders of broadband and satellite ensured he'd kept tabs on Columbia Walker's career. So he'd heard how she'd turned down several lucrative big studio projects to produce and star in a movie of her own, a book adaptation. Columbia had, it seemed, returned to her independent roots and an early cut of "Personal Assistant", the debut feature from her new company, had played to critical acclaim among aficionados at the recent Sundance festival. However, the movie was still months from whatever general release it could secure and possible distributors seemed unsure how to handle it.

The letter, in her own hand, not typed, read disarmingly frankly. If Jon wanted to know – and Columbia could quite understand why he might not – what the film was about, he was warmly invited to a private screening in New York a couple of days hence. Plane ticket and accommodation paid, of course; she did so hope he'd attend. He might be pleasantly surprised, Columbia was sure he'd find her a different, altogether nicer person and she'd like to express her gratitude to him for inspiring her career change.

Jon took the flight. For a start he reasoned a free return ticket to the Big Apple was not to be dismissed out of foolish pride, he was bigger than that. As for his feelings toward his former employer, while not yet warm they'd mellowed with time and, niggling away in Jon's self-conscious, remained a stubborn sexual attraction, fuelled by the memory of their last encounter.

Outwardly she'd certainly changed, that was for sure. 'Very Nanci Griffiths,' he observed dryly of Columbia's new '50s-style print dress. No more than smidgeon of makeup, contacts traded in for round, steel-rimmed specs, a ponytail and – good grief! – short white socks and low heeled Mary Janes. Out with the Tinsel Town power-dresser wardrobe and in with wholesome Mid-Western girl-next-door attire.

'Shouldn't Toto be around here somewhere?' he grinned.

Relaxed and cheerful, Columbia returned the smile. 'Yeah I know,' she conceded, 'short of pierced cyberpunk it's as near as I could get to the opposite of the old image. Come in,' she added expansively, ushering Jon through the door of the small review theatre. 'I've block-booked this for review screenings to try and drum up some interest with the big multiplex chains

126

but this afternoon we've got the whole space all to ourselves. Fortunately its remote controlled so I guess I'm both host and projectionist.'

'You sell popcorn too?'

She laughed again in response. 'I guess a mutual hatred of junk food was one of the few things we used to have in common.'

'Things change,' allowed Jon easily.

'Glad to hear that,' said Columbia, sitting herself next to him, 'Hey, great, back row banquettes, just like in high-school. Perhaps after seeing my movie there'll be something else we share?'

Jon's brown eyes betrayed no clue as to his thoughts. 'Make or break,' thought Columbia and began the movie.

Fifteen minutes later Jon was beginning to glean what she might mean. 'Brave choice of subject,' he whispered, 'no wonder the distributors are wary.'

'Yeah, even the trendy art houses, but I always knew it would be tough,' agreed Columbia, 'in a post-feminist world not many people want to admit some women might actually enjoy getting a spanking, too many folks confuse that with violence against women or...'

'Think anyone into is a pervert,' Jon concluded.

'Exactly,' sighed Columbia, 'I didn't know myself until, well you know,' she clutched his hand and felt a thrill of elation when he held on to her palm.

Jon watched engrossed, the film was obviously low budget but professionally lit and artfully shot. The actors, despite being unknowns, bought a rare commitment and authenticity to their roles. Columbia had, in a courageous sink or swim career gamble, cast herself as the lead, a submissive young PA anxious to find someone who would fulfil her fantasies.

Jon felt his heart beat faster, as, in a defining dream sequence, the heroine graphically imagined herself being disciplined by her boss. Columbia imbued the role with complete credibility, first apprehensively locking the office door then, with a long, smouldering look at the handsome older man, lowering herself over his desk. Slowly, sensually she raised her skirt to reveal slender, black stocking-clad legs and perfect alabaster cheeks bisected – but not obscured – by the skimpiest of lingerie.

As her on screen manager eagerly smacked the proffered buttocks, Jon found himself fervently wishing himself in the man's shoes. Tightness began to constrict his groin, he felt overheated, a hand slid across his thigh to his crotch.

'Hmm, looks as if this scene is definitely having an affect on my test audience,' whispered Columbia teasingly. He felt her warn, sweet breath on his cheek, smelt her perfume.

'So,' she continued seductively, expertly unzipped his jeans and sliding to the floor in front of him, barely visible in the flickering light, 'I can't let you sit there in discomfort, let's see if we can take care of that.'

Transfixed, Jon sat watching Columbia's bottom bounce and ripple on the silver screen as the punishing palm burnished that delectable derriere. He gasped as in reality her hot little mouth gently engulfed his cock; hands skilfully stroked his balls; darting tongue ran the length of his member. Ramrod straight, his cock felt as if it were about to explode, teased by sensations both tactile and visual.

'Columbia I'm…' he began, trying to push her head away.

Momentarily she halted her oral ministrations and looked up

'Gonna come? No problem, honey,' and dipping her head she took him deep in her mouth and swallowed long and hard.

Luckily the next two scenes were mainly dialogue which gave Columbia, smiling like the cat who'd got the cream, a chance to resume her seat and Jon, still on cloud nine, the opportunity to recover a little of his composure. All too soon the final reel reached what was clearly the climatic – in every sense – scene. Wearing nought but knee-high boots and a halter top, Columbia's character was spanked by what was obviously the man for her; someone who understood submission needn't mean subservience, that equality can encompass difference.

Feeling her grip on his hand tighten, Jon looked at his host. Eyes shining, she was clearly aroused by her own work, still mentally occupying the character on screen. Time to repay the compliment, he thought.

Deftly Jon slid his hand up her skirt where, meeting no resistance, he gently parted her thighs. The minx! Columbia accidentally – or more likely by design – wasn't wearing knickers. Softly, he stroked her thighs teasing his fingers through her downy, pubic hair, quickly detecting the wet slick of arousal. Sliding into the kneeling position she'd occupied not 15 minutes before he lifted and spread her thighs, Jon bought his mouth down to kiss the honeyed portal, tongued her clit, finger-fucking her tight vagina. Columbia began to moan in pleasure, surrendering to the simultaneous pleasures of voyeuristically enjoying her own spanking, while having him expertly go down on her.

Facing away from the screen, Jon couldn't see her celluloid character smile blissfully as she slid her hand down to slyly masturbate while being spanked by her beau. That the real Columbia should come noisily, joyfully, just as the film ended was just a fortunate coincidence. After which, Columbia knelt a touch precariously on the folding seat while Jon, quickly but most satisfactorily to both concerned, took her vigorously from behind.

Then, straightening themselves up, Jon and Columbia adjusted their dress and left the picture house arm in arm in search of a coffee over which to discuss their future.

Alistair's Hobby
by Beverly Langland

Alistair's locked in his bloody den again! Not that Nadine minds so much. She's grateful he has a hobby to keep him occupied. It allows her to keep doing what she always does – whatever she likes. Truth is, their marriage hasn't turned out quite as she expected. She thought marrying an older man the right thing to do, thought Alistair would be a guiding hand. Though she also misguidedly thought that being older he would be more sexually experienced. He wasn't, particularly. It was her own stupid fault for playing coy right up until their wedding night. She was good at playing with men, but this time it had backfired. Alistair turned out to be a kind and gentle lover. Not her type at all. She had thought him more of a man. Man enough to keep her under control, to control her wayward tendencies, to cut her loose from her so-called friends who led her astray. Not that Nadine needs much encouragement. She is a natural flirt. Yet even Nadine senses her behaviour is getting out of hand. The neighbours are talking, don't like how she leaves Alistair alone while she swans off for a night out with the girls. She loves him but she just can't help herself. All those hard bodies, those young studs. Handsome studs like Paul – keen to please, keen to get inside her knickers. And Alistair makes it easy for her. He spends night after night in his workshop, has recently taken to redecorating the spare bedroom, and now calls it his den. God only knows what he's doing in there with all the banging!

Playing with trains no doubt. She's curious but Alistair keeps the door locked.

Well, you play with your trains, darling, and I'll find something else to play with. Maybe Paul? Maybe tonight? Nadine tiptoes down the stairs, but Alistair surprises her in the hallway, places his hands around her waist while she's stretching for her coat. "Off out?"

She turns, smiles sweetly. *He's like butter in my hands.* "You don't mind, do you?"

"Only that you look like a tart."

"Alistair! You don't mean that?"

"But I do!"

Alistair holds her by her elbow, briskly marches her up the stairs into the spare room – into his den – catching her once or twice when she stumbles in her ridiculous heels. Nadine casts her eyes furtively around the dark room, looking for clues as to what Alistair expects of her, what he intends to do. There isn't much to see – no trains, no model cars. The room reminds Nadine of a small old-fashioned gymnasium. The only items are some sort of wooden contraption to one side and a large cabinet set against the far wall. Wooden climbing bars spaced at regular intervals furnish the other walls. At least Nadine assumes they are climbing bars. Alistair walks to the cabinet, opens a drawer, withdraws what appears to be a wooden ruler. Nadine's face drains of colour as she looks on apprehensively.

"Hands on your head." His voice is full of purpose now, his distinguished features set into a look of determination – hard, stony-faced. Nadine has a sudden flashback to school, of Mrs Jones, her head teacher, reprimanding, making her stand in the corner of the room while the other girls snigger. Alistair uses the exact same tone – uses a teacher's voice. It is full of disappointment.

"Alistair, don't be silly."

"Hands on your head!" His jaw stiffens as he swipes her exposed thigh with the flat of the ruler, making her start. Nadine quickly obeys, places her manicured hands, painted

131

fingernails uppermost, on top of her head. She feels silly standing in front of Alistair like this, but she keeps them there all the same. She has never seen her husband so angry.

"Now, what were you saying about going out?"

"A quick drink with the girls, that's all."

Alistair studies her, walking around her slowly. He is a big man. Even in her heels, he is several inches taller. She watches, a little dazed as he fumbles with the buttons of her blouse, then, irritated with his slow progress, rips apart the folds of cloth. Nadine gasps, feels embarrassed when her breasts fall free, when he reveals she isn't wearing a bra. He shakes his head, tuts mockingly, yet quickly has his hands on her breasts, roughly fondling them, kneading them, stretching them. "Get these pierced," he states flatly, flicking one of Nadine's nipples with the end of the ruler.

"Alistair, what's going on?"

"I've had enough of your antics. I'm reining you in."

"But Ali, darling …"

"Quiet!" He flicks her other nipple, then while Nadine's breast still reverberates, he swipes viciously with the ruler. Nadine cries out in pain, looks to her husband beseechingly. Alistair doesn't flinch. Quite the opposite – he swipes her other breast equally harshly. "Ow! Stop that."

"I said quiet!" Alistair strikes her breasts again, leaving two broad marks on her otherwise perfect skin. Nadine bites her lip to stifle her cry. She cannot believe what is happening, cannot believe Alistair is treating her this way. She glares at him, but for once he holds her eye. She feels his hands on her bottom, undoing the zip of her skirt, releasing the material, letting it fall to the floor. The cool air of the sparsely furnished room washes across her buttocks. "No panties?" he chides.

"Honey, you know this skirt clings. It looks wretched with underwear."

"Your friends wouldn't like that?"

"They can be so bitchy. You know what girls are like."

"I know what you're like."

"Darling, what's all this about?"

"It's about setting boundaries."

"I don't understand."

"Don't worry, you will. Turn around."

Hesitantly, Nadine obeys. Shortly after, Alistair is fondling her bottom, massaging the cheeks, rudely pushing, pulling them this way and that, as if assessing their condition, their firmness. Then, just as abruptly as before, he strikes her with the ruler. Alternating between the cheeks, first one and then the other. Three stokes on each. The pain isn't nearly as bad as when he swiped her breasts, but it is bad enough. Bad enough to make her buttocks smart. Bad enough to bring tears to her eyes.

"Alistair, don't."

"Hurts when someone betrays your trust, doesn't it?"

Alistair shifts position to face her, staring into her green eyes, smiling, perhaps sensing her apprehension. "Who's Paul?"

Nadine blushes. "Anne's friend," she says quickly.

"Not yours."

"No. I hardly know him."

"Yet his number is in your phone."

"I ..."

"Chest and bottom out," he scolds.

Nadine responds, immediately pushing her breasts out before her, arching her back to offer her bottom. She feels ridiculous in this contrived position, but it seems to please her husband – the way her position forces her breasts to stand to attention. And she is desperate to distract him, to gain time to think.

"Good," he coaxes, "just a little further." He cups one of Nadine's breasts, takes her nipple between thumb and forefinger, places his other hand on her bottom. "That's a good girl," he encourages her. He gently squeezes Nadine's nipple, begins to lightly spank her buttocks as she shifts position. Without fully knowing why, Nadine strains to offer her bottom further, to push her breasts forward, coaxed somewhat by Alistair's firm grasp on her nipple. Alistair suddenly stops spanking, runs his hands over Nadine's body, along her back, her stomach, as a judge might with a pedigree dog as he checks for posture, for bone structure. "You're a prize bitch, you know that?"

Nadine is about to say something, to spit something vile and nasty in retaliation, then remembers Paul. She bites her lip. For once she keeps silent. Alistair notes her restraint, smiles. "Good girl," he states, ruffling Nadine's hair affectionately. Nadine is appalled how elated her husband's praise makes her feel. She is dismayed how proud she feels having stood firm while calmly accepting his callous manhandling. Only moments before, he had been sadistically abusing her, now, for whatever reason, she adores him for it. What is wrong with her? Why isn't she struggling? Why isn't she pleading? Why isn't she running? Most of all, why is she so excited?

"Paul has a big prick?"

"I wouldn't know!"

"But you've thought about it haven't you? Perhaps sneaked a look?"

"No!"

"Were you meeting him tonight?" He takes both Nadine's breasts in his hands, starts to stroke, squeeze and pinch her rather roughly, coaxing her to accept his punishment, teasing her to push herself forward into his hands. He runs one hand along her flat stomach, around to her bottom, giving the cheeks a couple of gentle slaps before sliding his hand between her legs. She is wet. The feel of his big rough hand against her naked flesh excites her further. "Nice?" he whispers.

Nadine can do nothing but nod while Alistair continues to caress her, bringing his hand back to her breasts occasionally, squeezing them in his vice-like grip. Nadine bites her lip, fighting her humiliation as she stands submissively, allows Alistair's hands to roam freely. She stares into his grey eyes, can clearly see his excitement. Nadine is equally as excited, knows Alistair can tell also.

134

"Let's move on," Alistair states, breaking their locked gaze. "When did you last fuck Paul?"

"I haven't."

"But you intended to. Tonight maybe?"

"No, I …"

"I know when you're lying, Nadine!" He taps Nadine's breasts with the ruler. "Better you admit it now."

"He's just a friend."

"Anne's friend?"

"Yes. No."

"So you did lie?"

"I thought you might not understand."

"Oh, I understand – slut!"

"Alistair, he's just –"

"Right, chest out, shoulders back." He is in bossy teacher mode again. Nadine adjusts her position, her breasts bouncing obligingly as she thrusts them forwards, bracing herself for the expected onslaught. Alistair admires her for a moment, letting her strain to hold position. It is difficult for Nadine to comprehend why she is striving to please him so, when he obviously intends to make everything difficult for her. What possible motivation can she have for helping him? None, except the fire gradually building between her legs. The more she degrades herself, the hotter she seems to burn. She is already past questioning her actions. She just needs to stoke the fire!

"No moving, keep still," Alistair instructs as he readies the ruler in front of her. "Understand slut?"

Nadine nods.

"Good Girl." There it is again. That sense of pride.

Nadine finds her enforced submission surprisingly exciting. Alistair gives her a ferocious swipe with the ruler across the top of one breast. She groans loudly, unable not to yell out but she remains motionless, as instructed.

"So you were just flirting?"

"Yes."

He lands a blow to her other breast, this time catching her

nipple. Nadine bites her lip hard, trying not to make a sound.

"Fantasising, get yourself excited?"

"Yes."

Another blow. She badly wants to maintain what little dignity she can muster. Yet, Nadine knows she will soon break if Alistair continues as he has started. Thankfully, she is to get some respite. He returns the ruler to the drawer. "Tell me about the other men you flirt with." Alistair turns to face her. Nadine is surprised to see he has an obvious erection.

"Alistair, there isn't ... I don't ..."

"Liar! Well, if you insist ..."

"Please, not the ruler again."

Alistair smiles. "Oh, I agree."

He leads Nadine by the arm to a large wooden structure on the far side of the room. Now she is closer, Nadine can see it more clearly. It reminds her of the vaulting horses used in gymnastic classes. She stares at Alistair wide-eyed. Again he smiles, "My little hobby." Pressing between her shoulders he silently persuades Nadine to bend over the wooden contraption. She yields willingly. The beam is set at a slight incline, so once bent her head sits lower than her bottom. She feels the blood quickly rushing to her head. Alistair taps at her heels with his foot, indicating she should place her feet next to the thick legs of the horse. She obeys, again willingly, spreading her legs wide until she feels her ankles touch the coarse wood. Alistair clamps her ankles in place. Nadine feels the cold metal of the shackles against her skin, doesn't need to move to test their effectiveness – she isn't going anywhere until released.

Once securely fastened, Nadine grows decidedly apprehensive. Spanking is one thing, but Alistair's peculiar set-up indicates he has something altogether different in mind. She fights the urge to struggle, knowing it is already too late. Despite her anxiety, Nadine's helplessness continues to excite her. As she gradually comes to terms with her confinement, Alistair passes a strap around her chest, pinions her to the beam, pulling so tight she can hardly draw breath. He pulls her arms behind her back, ties them at the wrists. She can do nothing now but wait. The power he holds over her – power to do as he pleases arouses her beyond reason. For once Alistair has complete power over her. Will he be benevolent? Will he be harsh – abuse her? From what she knows of her husband, she assumes the former. Not surprisingly then, she feels no panic, only a strange sense of inevitability. Behind, she can hear strange noises as Alistair fumbles in the cupboard. She cranes her neck in an attempt to see what he is doing. It is no use; all she can see is the green-painted walls. Not her choice of colour at all. Suddenly Alistair moves to the front and Nadine hears herself scream involuntarily. Alistair holds a birch rod in his hand.

"Exquisite," he exclaims in delight, "you actually sound frightened."

"Alistair, please. You can't …"

"Oh, but I can Nadine, I can." She watches as he flexes the rod between both hands before swishing it through the air dangerously close to her exposed bottom, feels the cold rush of air as the rod passes her flushed skin. Alistair is testing his arm. Alarmingly, he suddenly looks strong, muscular, much as she likes her men. Nadine grows so nervous her saliva starts to overwhelm her capacity to swallow. Alistair notices, runs his finger across Nadine's lips, wiping the excess away thoughtfully. "Exciting, isn't it?"

"Alistair, have mercy!"

"Let's face facts darling, it's no more than you deserve."

"Please …"

"Confess your sins, Nadine, and I'll go easy on you."

"I've done nothing!"

"Nothing? You haven't been cavorting around town without underwear? Well?"

"Not cavorting …"

"Well, what do you call it?"

The reality of her situation hits Nadine like a falling brick. Alistair clearly intends to beat her for her way she has treated him. She senses none of the playfulness or restraint he expressed earlier. The condescending teacher's tone is gone. Alistair's voice is now deep and sinister, for the first time Nadine feels a tinge of genuine fear. Alistair has her completely exposed and at his mercy. Excited or not, how can she have been stupid enough to get herself into this situation?

"I want you to count out the strokes and thank me after each one. Do you understand?"

"Please don't do this," Nadine pleads from beneath her mask of hair, but all she can hear is muffled gobbledegook, her heart is beating so loudly. Alistair hears nothing, or chooses not to. Instead of mercy, she feels the vicious bite of Alistair's rod across her backside. She cries out in pain, in anguish.

"I asked if you understood."

"Yes!" Nadine hollers angrily, then nods as vigorously as her restrained condition allows. The first stroke was more painful even than she had imagined.

"Well?"

"One. Thank you Alistair."

"My pleasure, Nadine," he replies, sounding as polite, as casual as if she had just thanked him for opening a door. "Though a little louder please." He brings the cane down hard across her buttocks. "Ow!"

"Tut, tut," Alistair hisses sarcastically, "we'll never get to ten at this rate."

"Ten?"

"One for each night you left me here, alone."

Again, Alistair brings the cane down hard across Nadine's exposed flesh. This time she manages not to cry out. "One! Thank you, Alistair," she states bitterly, unable to keep the loathing from her voice.

"I don't care for your tone," he replies, "Again!"

Nadine groans inwardly. There is only one way out of her predicament and she doesn't fancy the prospect one iota. She braces herself for the next strike. When it comes, she calls out as Alistair instructed, but it takes all her will to keep the hatred from her voice. "One! Thank you Alistair," she says flatly.

"Much better."

After seven strokes, Nadine's buttocks are on fire; the searing heat burns into her young flesh, scorches its way deep within. Tears stream from her eyes. There is no way she will endure another six strokes. There is no way anyone can endure such concentrated pain.

"Five! Thank you, Alistair." She prays he will stop, willing him with all her might to forgive her. *Please stop! Please stop and I'll do anything. Anything*! Miraculously, Alistair does stop. Nadine hears the rustling of clothes, and then feels his hardness pressing against her sore flesh as he slowly runs the tip of his erect prick over her buttocks, between her bottom cheeks. She has thought about anal sex many times, but not now, not like this! She'd rather feel the pain of the rod. Then, as suddenly as it appeared his cock is gone and, despite her panic, Nadine feels an inexplicable sense of disappointment. She has little time to reflect on this conundrum as the next blow lands across the stinging globes of her buttocks. In her confusion, she almost forgets to call out the stroke. "Five! Thank you Alistair," she shouts hurriedly, before realising her mistake. "Six!" she corrects quickly. Her stomach turns in dread. She should have kept quiet. What if Alistair makes her start over?

"Five." Alistair admonishes quietly.

"Yes, five! Thank you, Alistair, thank you," Nadine replies, genuinely thankful, though she is disgusted with herself for kow-towing to the sadistic bastard.

"Six! Thank you, Alistair." Nadine's bottom is so hot, she is sure that if she looks back she will see flames. It is a fire that not only scorches her outer flesh but also burns deep into her sex. Despite the pain, she knows she is soaking between her legs. Nadine feels humiliated, used, is completely at his mercy, yet, as disgusted as she feels, the idea of being at Alistair's mercy still excites her! The paradox is plain to see, but Nadine is slow to comprehend. He hurts her and she likes it. Not likes, exactly, but still it arouses her. This isn't happening. She must be dreaming. The pain from the next stroke proves otherwise.

"Seven! Thank you, Alistair." What will he do to her next? Force his penis into her bottom?

"Eight! Thank you, Alistair." Yes, he will force his penis into her tight virginal bottom. The idea both appals and fuels her excitement. Her pussy is a raging inferno, hotter than her punished flesh can ever be. She pushes her bottom out to meet the next stroke, an effort to stoke the fire, not caring about the pain any longer.

"Nine! Thank you, Alistair." She badly needs to feel someone or something inside her – anything to quench the unbearable heat between her legs. Then, as suddenly as it had started, it is over. "Ten! Thank you Alistair." *Yes, thank you Alistair.*

There follows a long pause during which Nadine can do nothing but wiggle her buttocks – a vain attempt to disperse some of the heat. After such intense activity, the lull becomes an exquisite torture in itself, stoking her arousal to new heights. She feels tempted to cry out, to goad Alistair into getting on with whatever abuse he plans next. Anything would be better than her slow smouldering torment. She doesn't – though the thought of rebellion and reprisal sends a bolt of electricity to her pussy. Nadine is so aroused now, just thinking about further punishment draws her closer to climax.

"Well, slut, are you sorry?"

"Yes, Alistair."

"So you should be." Suddenly, she feels cold lotion on her scorched bottom. Is Alistair deliberately tormenting her? He spreads a generous quantity over each buttock, works the liquid well into the flesh. Nadine finds the drawing of heat nearly as painful as the actual beating, the application of the balm obviously important to Alistair as he invests considerable effort rubbing the lotion into her skin. Soon it becomes clear why as his fingertips touch, and then explore, her rear opening. Alistair spreads Nadine's rosy cheeks wide, runs his thick stubby fingers lightly over the crack of her bottom, concentrating on the wrinkled, tightly closed opening. Then, without further warning he slips a finger inside.

Nadine jumps in surprise, though the sensation isn't unpleasant. After all, she occasionally does the same while masturbating, although Alistair's digit feels decidedly bigger. She closes her eyes, enjoys his gently probing finger, trying to suppress her rising feeling of guilt, her feeling of shame as he explores deeper. After some minutes, Alistair stops, withdraws his finger. Nadine, lost to the illicit pleasure, hears herself groan with disappointment.

Alistair releases the strap around her bound wrists. "Reach back and open yourself for me," he commands, the excitement in his voice now almost at fever pitch. Nadine's mind is in turmoil. She – they – have wanted this for some time, but now it's as if he's forcing her, as if the choice is his alone. The sadistic bastard clearly intends to do it his way – she can feel his hardness bobbing against the heated flesh of her bottom. Does he actually think she will assist him? She feels his prick nudge against her opening and she lets out a low guttural moan, realises she is equally aroused, isn't sure she wants him to stop. The burning fire between her legs needs quenching – and quickly. Incredulous at her own submission, she reaches back, holds her buttocks open.

Once spread wide, Alistair continues to ream her rear hole. His other hand grasps his member, strokes it as he edges the throbbing hardness ever closer to Nadine's virgin orifice. Nadine can feel the bulbous end nudge between her cheeks and, to Alistair's obvious delight, she moans aloud. For a long moment, nothing changes. She thinks he has relented, perhaps only intends to ejaculate over the sore and reddened globes of her bottom. Despite her earlier apprehension, she feels disappointment at his lack of forcefulness. He is master now, why doesn't he take her? She pushes her bottom backwards against the head of his cock, letting him know she wants him. All of him.

"You're a slut, Nadine."

"Yes, Alistair, I'm a slut."

Alistair presses into her. She feels herself slowly open, her rear hole expanding until the head of his cock is snug inside.

Her muscles close tightly around the shaft. Alistair's groans are louder than hers, yet he hesitates before delving deeper. Nadine is thankful for that small mercy. She pants heavily while she gets used to the unfamiliar fullness. Then, slowly but with deliberation, Alistair edges inside her, a little at first, then pulls back before pressing again, equally slowly. He groans again, obviously enjoying the tightness of Nadine's unexplored depths. As Alistair slowly gains momentum Nadine revels in the novelty of the new sensation. Soon, she feels comfortable enough to want more than Alistair gives.

She wishes he'd get a move on. Fuck her like she deserves to be fucked. Use her like the slut she is. Again, she pushes herself backwards, this time with enough force to cause his testicles to bang against her bottom, any soreness now forgotten. At the next stroke, Alistair thrusts harder into her. She matches his forcefulness eagerly. "Yes, Alistair, yes." Alistair registers Nadine's signal. He quickly increases speed, ramming into his helpless wife with great abandon. Within seconds, they are both moaning, shouting abuse at each other and, with her hands now free, Nadine cannot resist reaching between her legs to seek her clitoris. She rubs frantically at the nubbin, as hard as marble beneath her fingers. She is dangerously close to orgasm now.

"Fuck me! Fuck my arse," Nadine shouts repeatedly, as she climbs ever closer to the peak of pleasure. She desperately wants to reach that holy summit, rubs her clitoris furiously, knowing if she continues she will be sore for days. Yet she doesn't care. What difference does it make now? Reaching behind with her free hand, she slaps Alistair's thigh in encouragement, goading him to greater effort as they both race towards the finishing post. She is almost there, almost there … and as she feels her orgasm overwhelm her, she contracts around his pounding shaft. It is too much for Alistair. Gasping, sweating profusely in an effort to keep pace with his young wife, he shoots his heated load deep inside her – just as her orgasm starts to ebb. Overtaken by this new sensation, Nadine is instantly thrown over another, higher peak. Her renewed shouts join Alistair's in a crescendo of animal howling as they both fall crashing into oblivion.

"I'm so sorry," Nadine whispers as Alistair releases her, holds her in his arms. "I promise I won't flirt again."

"Why not, my dear?"

"Because, because …" He waits in silence while realisation slowly dawns. "You want me to, don't you?"

Alistair leans over, kisses her furrowed brow. "Why the dilemma, sweetheart? You have your hobby and I have mine."

Lollycocks, Glory Holes And Bears! Oh My!
by Astarte

I love a fruity lollycock! So does Hyacinth! Sometimes we share one. Like when we've got Harry bared, nipple-clamped, spread-eagled and tethered on our double bed. After a suitably sensual spanking, Harry's lollycock is rampant, ready and throbbing; a glistening pearl of pre-cum at its tip. We lick his lollycock together, running our tongues up the hot shaft to take the pearl, meeting in a lascivious lezziekiss before taking it in turns to deepthroat the juicy morsel, tonguing and sucking till cumtime. Then it's guzzle and gobble time as we milk him dry and kiss again, our mouths full of cream, spreading his lotion all over each other's tits and then having him lick our breasts dry while he fingerfucks us both together. That's what we call an orgy – or what wild-card Harry calls "a high Two Pair!"

I leaned over Hyacinth's bed and pinched a nipple. I knew she would be tired after such a night of fun. My Harry had come to dine at our Lowndes Square pad in Knightsbridge, collecting a royal ransom in oysters, lobster and white wine from Harrods Food Hall on the way over. We had pigged out on seafood and Chardonnay before stripping down to our Agent Provocateur undies to play Dirty Dictionary. Win or lose, the result is always the same! If Harry wins, we flog his butt. If we win, we flog his butt! So it's a win-win situation! After that we all end up on our king-size bed bonking our brains out ... who said "Three's a crowd!"?

We never lose.

Harry tried that obvious old chestnut "Dick tater ... dictator" with a potato hanging on a string from his prick, and later, Hyacinth was quick to guess "Stopcock" before removing the large wooden clothes peg from his weapon and lovingly massaging some life back into it. Harry correctly divined Hyacinth's massaging my clit with her elegant big toe as "pussyfoot" but was obviously too excited by the spectacle to guess "rabbit hole" when I took Harvey, Hyacinth's lovetoy rabbit to her cunt and buzzed her to the night's first orgasm. The evening degenerated deliciously from that moment on.

But I digress!

It was high time to rise and shine because slave-driver Nyna had called to check we were packed and ready for our flight to Toronto. As Morning Glory's Fashion Director, she had booked us for a week's photoshoot in Ontario for their new 'Great Outdoors' Sporting Collection, to make the glossies in time for the London Fashion Week catwalk shows. So we were off to do a fashion shoot up in the Canadian backwoods and then at Niagara Falls.

Hyacinth peeped out from under her long lashes and squinted at the sunlight.

"Bounce your tits out of the sack, Sweetcheeks! We have to be at Gatwick in two hours, so shake a gorgeous leg, sweetie! Nyna says it gets chilly in early September up in the primeval woods where we're going, so I've packed us sweaters and jeans, gloves, rag socks and long johns."

Nyna had chosen a remote place called Aubrey Falls for the shoot, chartering a seaplane to fly us up into the wilds and landing us on a river called the Mississauga. Some lumberjacks were to collect us there and take us to their logging camp. As well as looking after us, they were being paid to provide a muscular 'bit of rough' for decorative background. Thinking of the possibilities was tiring me out already!

Our dyky slave-driver and her (very) personal assistant Francine collected us, and with her chosen photographer, the classy Carla, and Antoine, our camp hairdresser and make-up artist, we trooped out to Gatwick together in the company van, along with the crated clothes.

I was tired and sore when we boarded our plane. Darling Harry sure can tongue and groove a woman and he used everything he had on me last night – and then some! I came over and over, drenching his face several times. I love watching him lick his lips and smile like he just had a mouthful of hot fudge syrup.

"Hold the fort, Harry, darling," I thought. "I'll be back to exercise your hard cock as soon as I get away from all those horny lumberjacks!" I hoped they were horny anyway, and I guessed Hyacinth did too!

It's a long flight into Toronto Pearson so we overnighted at a downtown hotel on our arrival to be fresh for our trip up into Grizzly country the next day. But there was to be no rest for the wicked! Antoine en drab was soon Antoinette en drag and had us all high-heeling down to Mandy's famous Goodhandy's Club for their draggy Pansexual Night, where gurlz will be boyz and boyz can be Queen for a Night! So Nyna and her chums were a touch heavy-eyed and Antoine was looking distinctly wan when they dropped Hyacinth and me off at the Toronto seaplanes dock on Lake Ontario before they set off upcountry with all the gear in a rented van.

A chartered DeHavilland Beaver was waiting for us. Ernie, the cute-arsed pilot, introduced himself and his navigator Arnold. They helped us on board, very free with their hands on our butts. Cheap thrill, but hey, I'm into thrills of any kind on these tedious trips.

We got settled in and were soon skimming out across the lake and up into the blue. Ernie explained that he takes off and lands on only one float as it cuts drag on the water. He mouthed a lot more techno-crap but all I wanted to hear was how long his dick was and how long it would take me to yank it out of his pants once we are airborne.

His answer came quickly. He glanced back and winked so I leaned forward, touched his arm and pointed at the scene

146

below. It was instant electricity

Ernie looked at Arnold. "Take the controls, Arnie and Hyacinth can take my seat, but don't let her touch anything! I'm going back to get better acquainted with Layla."

He clambered out of his seat and into the back beside me, helping Hyacinth into the front at the same time. He turned and we looked into each other's eyes. The beacon was working between us. He reached over to undress me. I raised my arms cooperatively to help him get my sweater off and of course I'm bra-less. He appreciated the view, and playfully pinched my tits. It was cramped up there but with my energetic help he had me starkers in no time.

I wasn't wearing any knickers and he cupped my cunt as I slithered out of my jeans! I was so hot now that he could have fried an egg on my hot pussy! But I was thinking more of roasting some hot Canadian Jerky!

I didn't wait long for a taste of sizzling sausage! He discarded his boots and pants, and he wasn't wearing under-shorts either (my kind of man). He had this hard-on that would have choked a horse. He sat down with it pointed to the ceiling, pulled me onto his lap and kissed me hard and long, putting his tongue deep in my throat for me to suck at hungrily! With his one hand on my tit and the other frigging my clit, I was going crazy with the combined sensations of tongue sucking, tit tweaking and clit stroking. God, it was so good! Sensing my need, he turned me to face the cockpit and lowered me onto his shaft and started fucking me, first long and slow, lifting my arse up and down on him and, as he got hotter and hotter, more furiously to my moaning and crying out. I came before he did, but he soon caught up with me.

"Get ready, Delicious, here it comes!"

He shot into me with loud grunts of passion and held me impaled, letting my tight pussy suck all the cream out of his magnificent shaft.

I slid to the floor and, taking his meat in my mouth, I licked the succulent mushroom head and ran my tongue down slick shaft to his balls. He slid to the edge of his seat and I took his balls one at a time into my mouth, tonguing and sucking their warm roundness.

My aerial gymnast was beginning to moan again and I could feel renewed life in that worthy weapon. I took him deep into my mouth, sucked and pumped him with my hand and he went crazy. He lifted me up on his lap to face him and lowered me again onto his rampant cock. I rode him like a stallion, my hair wildly tangled all over our sweating faces. This time we came simultaneously in loud moans and cries of ecstasy! God, what a stud I had found!

Then he laughed. "You are now a member of the 'Mile High Club!' Arnie knows to take her up to 5, 281 feet; we give it an extra foot to be certain that we are over a mile high! Baby, you are something to dream about! I never had it so good."

Ernie squirmed beneath the pussylock I had on his key. "I gotta take over for a while and let Arnie initiate your friend into the 'Mile High Club' too! We'll get our clothes on and let them come back here. You can slide into Arnie's seat next to me. Baby, am I glad we got this run for your agency! This is a dream trip!"

It wasn't long before we heard giggles, whispers and frantic undressing behind us. Hyacinth and Arnold were getting it off to get it on … in seats that were still hot from Ernie's sexy arse!

We swapped again and fucked and sucked our way through the two hour flight. We were both ready to collapse from lack of sleep, but neither of us would have missed this trip for the world. We sat as couples now with me and Ernie in the cockpit (I know why they call it the "Cock Pit" now!) and Hyacinth and Arnold in the passenger seats.

Before long Ernie pointed out the ribbon of the Mississauga River he was going to land us on, and the dock where the lumberjacks would meet us. We watched the river grow bigger beneath us and then we were landing and coasting smoothly into the side of the dock where three burly hunks of muscle stood waiting. Built like tree trunks, they were wearing typical loggers' gear; denim pants, plaid shirts and heavy, steel-toed boots.

Ernie and Arnold jumped out and secured the plane to the dock, reached in for our bags and then helped us out with lots of lascivious touching on the way ... Ernie let me slide slowly down his body before releasing me. His eyes smiled into mine and gave me a crushing kiss. The lumberjacks' eyes were like saucers as they looked us up and down, obviously liking what they saw and wondering how we knew these pilots so well, having just arrived from London.

Ernie bid us goodbye, saying he would return in two days. His wink promised a fun flight back!

"Look after them! They've had a tiring flight!"

I waved my studman a tired goodbye.

We watched the Beaver take off and turned to the three lumberjacks who introduced themselves as Bernard, the foreman, Marcel the 'topper' and Jacques the cook.

Bernard's granite face cracked into a smile. "Call me 'Big Burly'. You call 'eem 'Topper', and Jacques, 'Flapjack'." His voice was a deep gravelly rumble

"Where is the restroom? we have to pee so bad our kidneys are floating."

Big Burly thought my question very funny. He gave a jolly belly laugh and pointed to the woods bordering the rough dirt trail leading from the dock.

"Go be'ind zee tree!"

"You gotta be kidding! No outhouse? No nothing but woods?"

"Zees eez ze backwoods, Mamselle! Eet eez very primitif," Big Burly rumbled in his sexy French-Canadian accent. "We wait on ze trail for you and zen lead you to ze camp!" That sexy smile appeared again. "Mais prenez garde! Beware ze greezlees!"

We decided we could wait till we reached the camp. The only nice 'greezlees' I knew, were in a Walt Disney movie.

We began to totter up the trail with the guys. Our high heeled boots, so elegant in the urban wilds of Knightsbridge, proved quite inadequate for Canada's real outdoors. I made no complaint when Big Burly lifted me up and cradled me to his chest and Hyacinth positively flew into Topper's brawny arms, leaving fat Flapjack to carry our bags. On the way, Flapjack bragged about the delights of his cooking and Big Burly told us about the knotty pine shower house he and Topper had erected specially for 'ze ladies'. We would soon discover that strategically placed knotty pine holes can be put to a number of unexpected uses.

The loggers had taken time off to greet us and were assembled in the camp lodge. They raised a cheer when Big Burly and Topper strode in bearing their human cargo. We had to shake a dozen hands the size of meat plates and drink a steaming cup of Flapjack's ever-available hot coffee before we were finally taken to our quarters.

"Ze woodland palace," Big Burly said, as he and Topper showed us into one of the four little log cabins made ready for our team. It was a simple room warmed by a glowing wood stove with two sturdy wooden beds, a table and chairs. A mirror hung above a sidetable, on which stood a pail of water and a dipper. Primitive, but Aubrey Falls is not Mayfair and at that moment those sturdy wooden beds looked more inviting than any fancy Claridges suite! We shushed them out, promising to meet up for dinner after the others had arrived in the van. We collapsed onto our beds and promptly fell asleep!

Our van duly arrived, and refreshed from that much-needed kip, we all met in the lodge for dinner with the loggers.

It was still early when Nyna reminded us that we were starting the photoshoot at daybreak and chivvied us all off to bed. We trooped out of the lodge, collected towels from our cabins and made for our little shower house. We undressed and were laughing and splashing each other with the makeshift shower spray when Nyna put her finger to her lips. We clammed up and heard snickers and low talk outside the wooden building. Two jacks were watching us through two large knotholes in the wall.

Sneaky, horny bastards! I didn't blame them for wanting to

see us starkers. All they had to look at during the summer was Indian squaws in the reservation trading posts, and each other's bare arses in the showers! Eye candy like Hyacinth and me, our lipstick dyke Nyna, her sweetie Francine and classy Carla would be a pleasing change from hairy knees and nuts.

Nyna has a devious down-and-dirty sense of humour. "Carry on as if they aren't there," she whispered. "Pose about and give them a thrill. We'll give those two horny wankers an eyeful now, and sort them out tomorrow after I've had a word with Big Burly. I've got a naughty plan! We'll leave them a painful memory they'll never forget!"

There was a wicked gleam in Nyna's eye as she began posing provocatively for the two secret voyeurs; sensually drying first Francine's and Carla's tits, then Hyacinth's and finally mine. Did I say "wicked"? By the time she got around to buffing up my boobs, her wicked gleam had turned to pure lust. Francine and Carla were in for a lively night in their shared cabin … so much for their early night – again!

The two covert knothole peepers had scarpered when we left the shower block and we laughed when Nyna told us what she had in mind for them as we walked back to our cabins.

She had obviously enjoyed touching us up for the voyeurs' benefit. Her lingering kiss when she left me at our cabin door was more a promise of things to come than a friendly goodnight peck. Future location photoshoots with her could be interesting!

Our photoshoot the next day at Aubrey Falls was exhausting. Big Burly and Topper took us through the woods to our location in a horse-drawn log wagon. Together with our admiring musclemen, the Falls made a dramatic backdrop for Carla's camerawork.

We paused at midday for a nice moose sandwich and hot coffee, while Nyna took Big Burly and Topper to one side for a quiet chat about the unwelcome knothole peepers. I could see that the men were very angry at the news that someone had abused the good name of their small community, but then they began to nod in agreement with her, before finally roaring with laughter at her suggestions. Slave-driver Nyna kept us working through till dusk when Carla complained of insufficient light. On the way back to camp Nyna outlined the plan she had agreed with our hosts. Very naughty! I was going to love this!

We were tired and ravenous when we sat down with the loggers for dinner that night and did full justice to the freshly caught trout and juicy moose steaks that Flapjack served up for dinner. Afterwards, Hyacinth and I kept the boys drooling over our modelling stories while Nyna took the others off, ostensibly to pack up the clothes for our early morning departure but actually to prepare our painful surprise for the two peeping toms when they showed up again that evening to watch us shower.

I gave them an hour and then looked at my watch and yawned. "It's time for bed, Hyacinth! Come and shower with me before turning in!"

Two loggers glanced at each other meaningfully and leered lasciviously. I had identified our dirtybirds. The sting was on!

Antoine was waiting in drag in our cabin. As 'Antoinette' she was wearing one of my bras padded out with my knickers under one of my slinky dresses, fully made up and disguised beneath one of my fashion wigs. Very fetching! She told us that Nyna and the others were already hidden in the shower block, having taken down the makeshift clothes-line and prepared it with two slipknots, lining them up against the two knotholes in the wall. Carla was there with her cameras and Big Burly and Topper were hiding somewhere outside ready for the action.

I gave Antoinette an affectionate pat on that pert posterior she was so proud of.

"You're every Big Bear's wet dream!"

She tested her wiggle before I gave her an appreciative kiss and shoved her out of the door.

"It's time to go, Sweetie! You're on stage!"

Hyacinth and Antoinette walked over to the shower block, chatting loudly. Once inside they undressed slowly and provocatively, Antoinette wiggling her derriere invitingly at the peepholes while Hyacinth slid lacy knickers down her elegant legs and she rubbed lasciviously at her pussy.

"God I'm horny after a day with all those sexy lumberjacks. Too bad someone doesn't stick a dick through those knotholes for us to fuck and suck! I could happily polish off a big lollycock before bed!"

Two ogling voyeur eyes disappeared from the peepholes. They were transformed into 'glory holes' as two throbbing cocks were thrust through, hungry for promised attention.

"Ooh! Look what's for dessert!" Hyacinth cried. "Hot, luscious lollycock!" She knelt before one of the proffered cocks and, slipping the prepared loose slipknot around it, started fellating with gurgling noises of delight. Antoine needed no encouragement to follow suit and began to gobble greedily at the other.

Their energetic osculation brought the jacks to a frenzy. The girls sucked deep, frigging the disembodied shafts to explosive climax.

"Oh, God! I'm cumming!" the dirtybirds grunted almost simultaneously and spurted their hot loads between hidden lips.

This was the moment Nyna and Francine had been waiting for. They jerked the prepared line, pulling the slipknots tight on the now subsiding dicks and quickly tied both ends tightly together, trapping the cocks in their 'glory holes'. Shouts of pain and dismay greeted this action as they tried unsuccessfully to free themselves. They strained and grunted but their exertions only succeeded in tightening the tethers holding their dicks. All the while, Carla was clicking close-ups of the action.

The moment of humiliation had arrived. The tethered loggers were suddenly spotlighted as Big Burly switched on a floodlight to reveal them standing up against the pine wall, their pants ignominiously draped around their boots. Nyna stepped out of the shower block, followed by the others. Antoinette went over to the tethered pair, wiped a cumdribble from her rouged lips, took off the wig she had borrowed, and adjusted her slipped bosom.

"Aaaargh! It's a man! We've just facefucked a fag!"

The jacks looked around wildly as a roar of laughter and a round of applause broke out. The rest of the loggers were standing in a circle grinning at them.

Antoinette smiled contentedly. You will never know which of you got a gay blowjob, cos I'm not telling! But you know you enjoyed it as much as I did. And Carla here took some lovely photos as you came."

She knelt and planted a lipstick kiss on each of their lilywhite butts while Carla clicked away, and gave them a playful slap.

"Goodnight, you sweet thangs!"

A cheer went up from the onlookers as Antoinette turned and flounced dramatically off.

I have never seen big men cry before. The two tethered jacks were weeping in mortification and embarrassment at their plight and the onlookers were shedding tears of laughter.

Big Burly stepped out into the light. He wasn't laughing.

"Eez time for you to apologise to zee lovelee ladies for ze peeping 'oles or I leave you tied 'ere tonight for ze greezlees."

Two mumbled apologies were forthcoming and two very sore cocks were released so that the jacks could pull their pants up and slink away to their billet.

None of us got much sleep that night. We partied in the lodge with the loggers till the small hours. From there it degenerated nicely. Antoinette put my wig back on and wowed them with a tabletop burlesque routine. She quietly disappeared later, to reappear looking dishevelled and very smug about something at breakfast the next morning. I think Nyna and her coterie ended up the night initiating a couple of young loggers into the delights of flagellation, judging from the sounds of leather striking skin coming from the cabin next door.

As for Hyacinth and me, we spent quality time exploring the hidden parts of Big Burly and Topper. Or, to be more exact, they spent quality time exploring our hidden parts. They did a very thorough job of it too, and I now know why they made those cabin beds so sturdy!

The others departed in the van immediately after breakfast, leaving us to wait for our plane to arrive. At the appointed time Big Burly and Topper cradled us in their arms and carried us down to the landing dock and handed us over to Ernie and Arnie.

"Look after zem! Zey 'ave 'ad a tiring night!"

I waved my sweet muscleman a tired goodbye.

Ernie took one look at my face and knew exactly what Big Burly meant.

Men always do!

You Might Like It
by Penelope Friday

"Spank me?" She scoffed. "I'd like to see you try!"

"*I'd* like to see me try. That's the point."

There was an assessing look on his face, as his gaze dropped down to her bottom, curving suggestively under a skirt that covered her to mid-thigh. The look of assessment was returned by her, her head tilted to one side, her dark hair sweeping her shoulder.

"And what would I get out of it?"

He smiled.

"Try it; you might like it."

"Uh-uh. Not tempting enough yet. Persuade me more. What are you going to do for me in return?"

He hesitated. No doubt about it, he hesitated. Weighing up his options, she reckoned. Just as she was weighing up her own. Privately, she'd always had the odd fantasy about being smacked, but he didn't know that. He didn't need to know that. This way, she might get to try out two fantasies for the price of one. A bargain indeed!

She moved towards him, entwining her arms around his neck suggestively; pressing kisses against his cheekbone.

"I could suggest something," she whispered.

He was intrigued, she could see. Also, she could not help being wickedly amused by his anxiety. What on earth did he think she was going to ask him to do? Something so scandalous that he wouldn't be able to consider it without blushing?

"Go on then."

His hands had slid around her to fondle her arse, smoothing the silky material against her sensitive skin. She leaned her head on his shoulder and looked up at him.

"Well," she drawled slowly, "why don't we take things a little further? Why don't we … set the scene a little first?"

"What do you mean?" he asked.

So she told him…

He leaned heavily on the wooden desk, frowning slightly. Miss Fenella Grant had misbehaved too many times recently. She would have to learn that her behaviour was unacceptable. She would have to be punished. He looked around the book-lined study and waited for her to arrive.

She stood on the far side of the wooden door, smoothing out any possible creases in her tunic. Had she taken things too far? What would he say to her this time? What would he **do** to her? The tap on the door was timid – so light that she wondered whether he would hear her. But he must have been listening, because a stern voice called out in response.

"Come in."

Her fingers slipped on the door knob as she twisted it. Her palms were just the slightest bit sweaty. She rubbed them against her skirt and tried again. This time, the door opened, and she slid in to the room, standing just inside the door, hands clasped nervously in front of her.

"You wanted to see me, sir?"

"Yes. Yes, Fenella, I did. Come in further and shut that door behind you." She pushed the door to, and noticed a large, old-fashioned key in the lock. "Lock the door, and bring me the key."

"But, sir …"

"No!" He cut across her. "I give the orders in here, Fenella, not you. Lock that door immediately."

"Yes, sir."

She twisted the key. It creaked slightly as the lock turned.

Pulling it out, she found that it was lighter than she had expected: it looked so heavy and old. She held it in front of her, offering it to him while staying as far from his desk as she possibly could. He took the key from her hand, and placed it in a drawer. Fenella found that she could hardly breathe. It was just him and her in here now. There was no escape for her. She shuffled back a couple of steps, putting a gap between herself and him.

"Stand still, girl."

"Sorry."

He sat upright, and looked her straight in the eyes. His face was grave.

"Miss Grant, I have been hearing bad reports about you from every side. It appears that you have been misbehaving on a grand scale. I would be sorry to think that any of my students could be so disobedient without due cause. What have you to say for yourself?"

Fenella's heart was beating a little faster. He was *good* at this. How did he get to be so good at this? She could feel an answering throb to her heart lower down, between her legs. She hung her head a little.

"I'm sorry, sir. I didn't mean to be bad."

He rose to his feet, majestically.

"Didn't mean it? You come to me with more disgraceful – disgusting – reports than any other student before you, and all you can say is that you didn't mean it? Miss Grant, you will need to have a better explanation than that if you want to escape punishment."

Oh, punishment! She had been waiting for that word, and she felt a jolt in her stomach as he said it. The word lingered on his mouth like a promise. But she had her part to play, and she was enjoying playing it. She threw herself to her knees in front of him.

"Oh, sir. Oh sir, please don't punish me!"

"Have you been bad, Fenella?" he asked gently.

She looked up at him. He had walked around the desk and was leaning against it – right above her.

"Yes," she whispered.

"Very bad?"

"Very bad, sir."

"Then you must be punished, Fenella. Rules must be obeyed – do you understand?"

"Yes."

"Yes …?" He waited.

"Yes, sir," she corrected herself.

"And you will take your punishment like the naughty girl you are?"

"Yes, sir." (Yes, *please,* she thought.)

He bent down to her and put a hand underneath her chin. It was the first time he had touched her, and she shivered at the feel of his touch.

"You need to stand up, then, girl. Stand up and bend over the desk. But first, you will need to remove your panties – you **are** wearing panties, are you not, Miss Grant?"

"Oh, yes, sir."

"Then stand up and take them off."

She obeyed. Her hands slipped under her tunic skirt as she reached and pulled down a pair of skimpy white knickers. She held them in her hand and turned to him.

"What should I do with these, sir?"

"Put them on my desk. There." He pointed. "They will be directly in front of you when you bend over – a reminder, Miss Grant, of your sins. Are we clear about this?"

"Yes, sir."

"Bend over."

She leaned down across the dark wooden desk. It had a smooth surface, almost comforting against her cheek. She knew that with her motion, her tunic had lifted at the back, leaving her pale, tender bottom open to the elements – and to him.

"What are you going to do to me, sir?" she asked.

She felt a hand against her back, pushing her further down against the desk, so that her breasts were rubbing teasingly against its firmness.

"I am going to teach you a lesson, Fenella." His voice was gentler now, almost loving. He stroked the hand down her back, lifting the bottom of her tunic that little bit further when his hand reached it. "You understand that you need to be taught a lesson, don't you?"

"Yes."

"Yes –?"

"Yes, sir," she corrected herself obediently.

"Good. Remember, this is for your own good, Fenella." He permitted the first trace of laughter to appear in his voice. "I don't say that I get no pleasure from this, but – you know you deserve it."

"Oh yes, sir," she breathed.

His hand rubbed gently across her exposed bottom, leaving every nerve-ending tingling.

"You see, you've been a bad, bad girl."

He lifted his hand away and brought it back with a slap.

"Oh!" She couldn't help but exclaim; it was – it was a little painful but, at the same time ... she wriggled her arse a little, suggestively, begging for more.

"Keep still, Miss Grant."

The hand lifted and slapped again; lifted and slapped. There was a rhythm to the punishment that had her moaning against the desktop. Lift – slap – lift – slap.

"Sir!"

His hand paused on her bottom, smoothing the contours.

"Fenella?"

Lift – slap – lift – slap.

"Please...!"

"Please, what, Fenella? You know you deserve your punishment."

She arched her neck back, up from the desk, closing her eyes as she did so.

"Yes, yes, but sir..."

"What?"

"Fuck me," she moaned. "Please – please, fuck me. Please, I need you inside me."

The hand lifted and smacked once more.

"Miss Grant, I am ashamed of you. You are a student, I am a teacher. It would be most inappropriate to do what you suggest."

Slap – slap – slap.

"Yes, yes, I know – but please!" she whimpered, rocking back and forth, so that her nipples grew hard against the wood and she was wet, so wet, between her thighs. His fingers delved lower, noting the heat and wetness that she couldn't disguise.

"Oh, Fenella," he said, his voice a caress. "Oh, what a very naughty girl you are." One finger slipped inside her, pressing against her most sensitive places. "This is a punishment, Fenella. And you ... you're wet, you're giving, you're *begging* me, are you not, to make love to you?"

"Yes."

"Yes...?"

"Yes, sir!" The words were almost screamed as one finger became two, became three, thrusting in and out of her.

"Tell me what you want, Fenella. Tell me exactly what you want."

The fingers did not stop their movement for a second. He had no mercy.

"Oh, God." Without the slap of his hand on her arse, she could feel it tingling with need. With his fingers inside her, she could hardly think – hardly breathe – for wanting him. "Darling…"

His other hand was on her neck suddenly; his voice a savage whisper in her ear.

"But I am not your darling, am I, Miss Grant? I am your teacher, and I want to hear you beg. I want to hear every word of your *disgraceful* fantasies. I want to hear everything you've ever dreamed of me doing to you."

She wondered if he could make her come just from the sound of his voice. Perhaps she had not been the only one with this particular fantasy in mind. Her voice grew husky.

"Sir, I ... I've been such a bad girl." The fingers thrust hard inside her and she bucked under his pressure. "I have … I have dreamed, I have wanted you to …" Now his palm was on her bottom again, stroking the reddened skin. It was heaven. "I have imagined you doing just this to me, sir; spanking me until I couldn't take any more, until I screamed out for you …"

"Yes …?"

"Until," her voice sank to a low moan, "until I begged you to take me. Until I was so wet, so throbbing that I couldn't live without you inside me. And then you … you …"

"Tell me more."

"You pushed inside me, sir. You fucked me, over and over and over. I came, and came again, and it was your name – your name, sir – on my lips as I cried my desire aloud. Punish me, sir. I shouldn't have thought such things."

"Oh, Fenella, Fenella." He spoke with mild disapproval. "Oh dear. You are such a very bad girl."

The hand had gone from her neck, and she could hear the sound of him unzipping his trousers. It was unbearably exciting.

"Please, sir!" she begged.

"What did you say you wanted?" he demanded softly. She could feel his erection pressing against her. He was so hard. "Did you want me to do this …?" He thrust inside her and she moaned against the desk. "Did you?"

"Oh, yes, sir."

"And then," he continued, pushing further inside her, "you wanted me to …"

He was moving back and forth, gently at first but with ever increasing pressure until she too was thrusting against him, wantonly demanding and receiving pleasure.

"Yes, yes!"

"Yes …" His voice was lower, but his breathing too was fast now; she could feel that he was on the edge, close to tipping over.

"Yes," she echoed, and opening her eyes saw the sight of her pure white panties, two inches from her face.

It was the last touch. She came, crying out his name, just as she had told him. She felt him climax, too; throbbing inside her in a heavy breathing silence more sensual than any words could have been.

Later, much later, he spoke again, smiling.

"I think I could grow to like your fantasies, Fenella."

"Me too," she said, contentment etched across her body.

"Me too."

Victoria's Secret
by Virginia Beech

The sight of Alysha masturbating a half-naked girl to screaming orgasm in the stable hay room shocked Riding Mistress Maude.

To her horror, it was Guinevere who was the willing recipient of such lewd attentions from this darkly beautiful daughter of a deceased officer of the Bengal Lancers and his Calcutta concubine.

This was no surreptitiously stolen stable kiss. Guinevere's riding habit was hitched up over her creamy thighs, her knickers pulled down to bare her rounded bottom. It bucked in fetching provocation; the quivering cheeky curves clenching and unclenching in rhythmic fury, as she responded enthusiastically to Alysha's finger-fucking. Guinevere's voluptuous breasts hung free of their constricting bodice and Alysha was tonguing the lust-hardened nipples in hungry debauch.

Maude watched with gut-wrenching jealousy as Guinevere reached a knee-trembling climax beneath the finger squelching lasciviously within her cunt. She came, shuddering to the ecstatic surges that coursed from her inflamed clitoris to every nerve-tingling extremity of her body. Alysha knelt and buried her dark face to Guinevere's love-lips, her serpentine tongue lapping the sweet flowing nectar of her cum juices.

Guinevere was Maude's star riding pupil at Victoria's, the select Academy for orphaned 'Daughters of Fallen Heroes' situated off Berkeley Square in Mayfair. Formally opened by Queen Victoria when she was proclaimed Empress of India six years previously in 1876, the Academy charitably housed 30 indigent young ladies aged between 18 and 20, preparing them for a secure, if somewhat Spartan, spinster life as a governess.

An accomplished equestrienne under Maude's attentive instruction, Guinevere looked magnificent riding side-saddle in Hyde Park's Rotten Row each morning when they exercised the Academy's horses. Maude had long secretly lusted to possess her. In the confines of her bedroom above the mews stables behind Victoria's, she dreamed of tasting the sweet delights of her body, of baring Guinevere's bouncy breasts and sucking her nipples to excited hardness. She fantasized about Guinevere's hidden pearl nestling within that lush curly forest now so wantonly displayed before her, dreaming of her becoming her live-in stables assistant, when she would possess her in nightly Sapphic sensuality.

'Take me! Drink me! I love you!'

Guinevere's lecherous words galvanised Maude. She burst in, screeching like a banshee.

'Slut! Temptress! Harlot! Debaucher! Perverted whore! Defiler of womanhood!' she spat through white, bloodless lips.

She stooped and tore Guinevere's dangling knickers from her knees. 'The Governors will hear about your filthy perversion. I shall have you publicly thrashed and expelled for your obscene display of unnatural lust and debauchery.'

Minutes later, the girls were standing in dishevelled shock before Lady Jessica Cleveland, Victoria's appointed Headmistress. Maude had marched them from the stables in their hay-covered *dishabille*. Her screaming abuse, their disordered attire and Guinevere's torn knickers borne triumphantly aloft like a Mogul standard captured on a Punjabi field of battle, left no doubt as to what had transpired.

By the time they reached the Headmistress's study, Maude had worked herself into a frenzy of moral righteousness.

She threw her captured trophy onto Jessica's desk. 'Doing

165

it in front of the horses…Victoria's dishonoured!…Empire's Fallen Heroes defiled!…Calcutta concubine!…perverted harlots!….public thrashing!…expel them immediately!… inform the Governors!…'

She screeched on until lack of breath reduced her to rasping incoherence.

'That's enough, Miss Bullen,' the Headmistress barked. 'Please be silent!

Maude was one of the crosses Lady Cleveland had to bear when, prematurely widowed by the untimely death of her noble husband on an orchid collecting expedition to Papua, New Guinea, she had sold her spacious Belgravia mansion, bought a smaller property in Mayfair and accepted the gracious royal favour of appointment as Headmistress to the nearby Academy. Unfortunately, Maude came with the job. The founding governors were a cadre of feisty Generals; bemedalled veterans of Imperial forays into the dusty plains of India, the shifting sands of Egypt and the steaming jungles of Darkest Africa. General Sir George Bullen, VC., hero of Napier's Abyssinian Expedition of '67 and the Second Ashanti War of '74 was typical of these. His martial valour had lost him limb and livelihood, but gained him fame, if not fortune, and a place on Victoria's governing board.

Bullen had promptly engineered his daughter's appointment as Riding Mistress and now manoeuvred tirelessly to retire Lady Cleveland and appoint Maude as Head teacher.

Given the furore created by Maude's tempestuous progress from stables to Academy, Jessica had no alternative but to inflict the statutory punishment for 'immodesty'; a whipping and expulsion. Failure to do so would play into Bullen's hands; enhancing Maude's claim to be the Academy's strict guardian of maidenly morals and jeopardizing Jessica's position.

'What have you to say before I punish you?'

Alysha knew her fate. There would be no reprieve from ignominious expulsion. She would be one of Victoria's secrets. Could she save her sweetheart by accepting culpability, however?

'It was my fault, Headmistress. I seduced Guinevere. Expel me, but please don't punish her.'

Guinevere burst into tears at her sweetheart's brave words.

'That's not true! I'm to blame! Punish me, not her!'

The ulcerating acid of frustrated sexual desire and jealousy was now pumping corrosive poison through Maude's icy veins.

'Disgusting sluts! Purveyors of unnatural vice! Perhaps others are party to their filthy lust. My father will initiate an inquiry and expose the despicable moral laxity here under your Headship. The Board will…'

Jessica cut her short. This confrontation was moving onto dangerous ground.

'That would be unfortunate, Miss Bullen. You should be the last person to trumpet this outside these hallowed walls. It will reflect very badly upon you. As Headmistress, I must point out your own responsibility in this matter. You are solely responsible for stable discipline and this is not the first instance of such disgraceful behaviour there. You will remember that I expelled Estelle and Constance last year for similar turpitude in the stables. You appear to preside over a hotbed of unnatural sexual perversion. Perhaps I should recommend the Board to consider this sullied record and review your position.'

Jessica's words struck home. Maude sputtered into angry silence.

The Headmistress studied the two miscreants. 'As Miss Bullen has noted, your actions force me to whip and dishonourably expel you forthwith. I should assemble the girls and staff to witness your humiliation but I wish to spare our Riding Mistress the embarrassment of publicising such lamentable moral turpitude within her bailiwick. I shall therefore cane you privately and your expulsion shall become just more of Victoria's secrets.

She turned to their accuser. 'Leave us now Miss Bullen!

Return to your stables before any further lewdness occurs in front of the horses!'

Maude shot Jessica a look of thwarted hatred. She wanted to witness the caning, exulting in humiliating the girls, but had no answer to Jessica's barbed comments. She departed, slamming the door defiantly behind her.

With the Riding Mistress safely out of the way, Jessica moved rapidly to close the official expulsion proceedings and open her own secret agenda; an option that provided a very different future for the beautiful Alysha and Guinevere to that which they expected and Maude had intended.

She smiled wickedly at her secretarial assistant. 'Miss Downey, we have two more to add to our growing list of "Victoria's secrets"!'

The fair Caroline Downey was well versed in Academy punishment procedure, including the necessarily secretive nature of official expulsions.

Few days passed without a reported misdeed requiring the Headmistress's use of corrective cane upon bared bottom. The cane hung prominently on the wall beside Caroline's desk. It was Caroline's duty to prepare a pupil for chastisement, stripping her naked for "Punishment Undress", strapping her to the fearsome punishment horse in the corner, register the caning in the Governors' Punishment Book and have the tearful recipient sign the record.

Caroline herself was no stranger to the kiss of the cane. When Jessica found her secretarial work unsatisfactory, she would order Caroline to lift up her skirt, drop her knickers and bend over to present her plump, inviting posterior for punishment.

It was after just such an occasion four years previously that Jessica had first caressed her striped bottom with her cool hand before taking her into her arms and kissing away her salty tears. Exquisite pain had turned to exquisite pleasure, as Jessica's demanding tongue breached her willing lips. She had responded in a delirium of joy as that first exploratory kiss blossomed into a passionate embrace and a hand slid up the inside of her soft thigh to seek her waiting clitoris. Jessica's practiced touch to that throbbing button had quickly brought her to the ecstasy of her first orgasm. From then on, Caroline was her willing and adoring submissive and confidante.

Such blissful moments of extra-curricular caning took place now in Jessica's nearby home; euphoric occasions of clandestine sensuality which, like "Victoria's Secrets", were never recorded in the Academy's Punishment Book.

Jessica wrote out a brief note and gave it to Caroline.

'Take this expulsion order over to Main Hall and hand it to Duty Mistress. Instruct her to read it out to the staff and pupils. They will be congregating for Saturday Evening Prayers in 10 minutes.'

A teasing thought struck her as Caroline turned to leave.

'Who is Duty Mistress this weekend?'

Caroline giggled gleefully.

'Miss Bullen!'

Jessica allowed herself a self-satisfied smirk. 'How divine! How deliciously appropriate! And how convenient for us! That desiccated harridan can have her pound of flesh and pontificate at length on the sinfulness of exposing one's privy-pretties to horses, while we spirit these two love-birds away to our nest unseen! And we are not expected to return before Monday morning! Hurry back, dearest!'

Alysha and Guinevere looked totally bewildered. They expected a severe whipping and ignominious exit from Victoria's. The Headmistress and her assistant appeared to be reading from a different and altogether friendlier script. And what was "Victoria's secret"?

Jessica relished their bemusement. 'Contain your curiosity! Understand that I shall most certainly spank your naughty bottoms, but not here and now, and not in the way you expect! I am expelling you because Academy rules leave me no alternative. You brought this upon yourselves by allowing your physical desires to overcome you in a place where you could be discovered.'

The girls looked shattered.

'Your stupidity has led to your undoing and the loss of a secure position as governess. Your predicament is dire, your options few, your prospects bleak! No diploma; no references; no money; no future! You are "fallen women" destined for a clothing sweatshop in Whitechapel, or sex sold for pence behind the Alhambra in Leicester Square. Either way you face an early death from disease and physical abuse.'

Both girls looked at Jessica numbly. It was a sombre future.

'There is one very exciting but very secret alternative, however. But you must agree to place yourselves unconditionally in my hands and you will have to trust me implicitly.'

A look of desperate hope crossed their anguished faces.

'I have friends in high places! They will groom you for a new life far removed from a governess's lonely garret. They will prepare you for a *grande entrée* in a milieu where your feminine sensuality and personality will bloom like one of my late husband's exotic orchids. With our help, you will illuminate the most scintillating salons of London, Paris, Vienna and St. Petersburg. You will influence men of destiny. They will prostrate themselves before your bejewelled beauty.'

First Alysha, and then Guinevere began to sob, then cry and finally laugh with joyful tears.

'Yes! Yes!' Alysha choked. 'We place ourselves in your capable hands. Take us and mould us! Those salons sound deliciously decadent and luxuriously lively – unlike a cold garret tucked away in a draughty castle!'

'Good! You are obviously intelligent as well as beautiful! That's an excellent start to fame and fortune!'

Caroline returned to find Jessica hugging the two girls to her bosom.

'That Bullen bitch has read out your note. It's triumph to ashes for her!'

She giggled irrepressibly. 'She's leading the girls in prayer. I bet they're secretly praying for Lord Lust to clutch their virginal pussies when they visit the stables!'

'You forget your station, Miss Downey!' Jessica admonished with mock severity. 'I shall have to bare and punish *your* pretty posterior presently!'

She smiled in anticipation of that pleasing prospect as she ushered her charges out.

'Follow me! We can leave unseen now. It's just a short walk to my house and your new life...and that promised spanking!'

Jessica led them quickly down Curzon Street and into Brick Street, a nondescript narrow lane leading from Shepherd's Market to Park Lane. Stopping at No.21, she quickly hustled them in.

Jessica acknowledged the blond maid in tightly corseted, pink satin uniform who had opened the door and was in deep curtsy before her. She gave her hand to kiss.

'This is Clarissa, my adoring slut-maid. She will look after you until we whisk you off to Paris next week. Do not venture outside! It is imperative that no one from Victoria's sees you.'

She addressed Caroline. 'Put these star-crossed lovers in the Blue Room, tell them all they need to know about our lifestyle here and have Clarissa outfit them in something more provocatively alluring for a *Tableau Vivant* at our Sunday "Quilting Circle"!'

She laughed at the girls' mystification. 'You will remember I still have to chastise those dainty derrières of yours. You will discover you enjoy the painful experience!'

The girls dared to wiggle their butts provocatively.

'Run along with Caroline and Clarissa before I spank you here and now, you brazen hussies! I'll give you something to wiggle about tomorrow at "Quilting circle"!'

Jessica's extensive Mayfair residence hid a multitude of sins. It was outwardly unpretentious, giving no hint of its sumptuously furnished and exotically decorated interior. It doubled as her exclusively secretive "Ladies-Only" social club, The Amazons.

Given society's hostile chauvinistic attitude to female sexuality, her select club members were advisedly secretive about their relationships and energetic activities in the bedrooms there.

Sensually passionate lesbians fitted uncomfortably into a male dominated society, where docilely compliant wives were brainwashed into believing it socially acceptable for men to be cock-happy predators, while female orgasm was considered a dangerous physical aberration best cured by clitoridectomy. It was an era when refined ladies willingly surrendered their bodies to male gynaecologists who tested them for "abnormal arousal" by subjecting their clitoris to a clinical finger-fuck. The resulting orgasm was pronounced "deranged", and the priceless pearl surgically removed from its oyster.

Members met their lovers at No.21, allegedly for afternoon tea during the week, and "Ladies Quilting Circle" on Sundays. Earl Grey and quilting were perfect alibis for Sapphic dalliance in these safe and secure surroundings.

Quilting Circle was the club euphemism for Jessica's lesbian Spanking Sorority. She played horsewoman to visiting *femmes* on these occasions, wielding her stinging crop to their responsive flanks to the plaudits of their admiring dom lovers. It was also an opportunity to chastise the bared bottoms of offending maids, giving pleasure to the onlookers and, if truth be known, to the maids. This would be the perfect opportunity to discipline Alysha and Guinevere.

At 3 o'clock on Sunday, Caroline led Alysha and Guinevere into the crowded salon and stood them before Jessica in the centre of the room. Jessica was dressed in a severe black sateen corset with four suspenders holding red stockings taught against her firm thighs. She stood, legs apart, one gloved hand on the swell of her corseted hips, the other holding a long cane; an awesome demanding Mistress Domina. There was a murmur of appreciation from the expectant assembly as they surveyed their 'Mistress of Ceremonies' and her two beautiful girls.

Mistress Domina, tapped her thigh with the long cane. 'Why are you here?'

'We request punishment for immodest behaviour, Mistress!'

'What was that immodesty?'

' We fornicated in the stables in front of the horses, Mistress.'

Mistress Domina suppressed a smile. 'I shall cane you for your sluttishness! When I have reddened your bottoms to a pleasing hue, I expect you to demonstrate to us exactly what you were doing in the stables.'

Mistress Domina turned to the hushed and expectant audience. 'We shall initiate these supplicants into the mystic rituals of flagellation, transporting them through a threshold of pain to the ecstasy of sensual euphoria. You have witnessed their humble request for punishment. My cane will produce a painfully focused and memorable impact upon both their minds and bodies. Afterwards we shall enjoy their *Tableau Vivant* showing us what they were doing when they were interrupted. This time however, I promise no *coitus interruptus!'*

'Have them disrobe each other!' a voice called out imperiously. 'Let's see some lusty lewdness!'

Emboldened by the sexually charged atmosphere, Alysha smiled wickedly. She began a slow striptease, divesting herself of blouse, skirt and knickers to reveal the gentle curves of her bottom cheeks and petite patch of silky black hair that stopped above smooth, inviting cunt lips.

Turning to Guinevere, she undid her blouse and slipped it off her to reveal the ripe fullness of her voluptuous, firmly rounded breasts adorned with prominent red nipples that stood out from pink powder-puff areola. Entering into the spirit, Guinevere placed her hands on her head, raising her breasts in pendulous profile and wiggled provocatively as Alysha tweaked her tits to arousal. There was an envious sigh from the onlookers.

Unbuttoning Guinevere's skirt, she discarded it and slid her hands inside Guinevere's tight satin knickers, seeking the heat of her hidden cunt. Guinevere bucked against her hand as a fingernail stroked the slippery moistness of her conch, probing fleetingly for the sweet bud that throbbed therein.

Alysha knelt and sensuously eased down Guinevere's knickers. Her lips brushed lightly against her downy fleece. It swelled richly thick over the curve of her mound; a dense forest of copper curls. Her tongue flicked a second at Guinevere's altar of love in silent adoration before she rose and clasped her tightly to her bosom.

'I love you,' she whispered. 'I shall hold you tightly while Mistress canes us. We shall share the pain and the ecstasy together.'

Mistress Domina admired the raw beauty posed for punishment before her in sensual embrace. What magnificent creatures, she thought as she studied them. She admired the lithe Eurasian eroticism of Alysha's body. Her sweet pert bottom cheeks would be a joy to spank over her knee, she mused. She took in the long sweep of Guinevere's back that ended in the voluptuously rounded dimpled spheres she was about to cane.

She wondered irreverently what Guinevere could do with a dildo strapped to such strong Venus hips. She promised herself to discover the answer at a later date as she ran her hand lingeringly down her victim's body and then over her bottom. Guinevere flexed her hips and rump to the touch, enjoying the feel of Mistress's finger caressing her cheeks and the erogenous delights of her hidden button.

It was time to sting those buttocks. 'Hold her tight to your bosom, Alysha. This is intended to hurt.'

Mistress Domina whisked her cane, feeling its whippy springiness and enjoying the whirring sound of rattan cutting through air. Raising the cane over her head, she poised with the rod parallel to the ground as if parrying a sabre thrust to the head.

Crack!

She whipped the rattan down in a circular motion that cracked like a pistol shot to leave a fiery red streak across the tender underside curve of Guinevere's rounded spheres.

A burning fire shot through Guinevere's body. She bucked in involuntary reaction to the excruciating pain, grinding her cunt into Alysha's belly. Her scream was stifled by Alysha's kiss.

Mistress Domina struck twice more, placing each cut a cane's width higher than the previous one. Alysha felt each impact pass like a bolt of lightning through Guinevere into her own belly.

Guinevere's bottom was on fire from the three cuts across the tender lower curve of her cheeks. She writhed with pain, her pubis grinding roughly against Alysha's pussy as the agony flowed from her bottom to her belly and transmitted itself to Alysha.

Now Mistress Domina drew the cane back parallel to the three crimson stripes seared across the lower curves of Guinevere's ravaged cheeks. A wrist flick brought the cane sharply back and forward to strike in a whipping flash that bent the rod in its speed of delivery. A brilliant scarlet weal appeared across the centre of Guinevere's bottom. In strictly measured time, she cracked two more flicking parallel strokes, delivered with devastating speed and accuracy. Guinevere's breast heaved at the stinging pain, her breath coming in hoarse gasps. Perspiration poured down her face onto her glistening breasts, running in a rivulet between the twin mounds.

Her ordeal was over.

The onlookers sat in entranced silence. For one couple the unfolding scene had been too much. Their skirts were hitched up to their waists and glistening fingers rubbed furiously at each other's clits.

Mistress Domina moved round to cane Alysha's tender cheeks. After a lingering caress of her target, she unleashed a similar six cutting strokes upon her rounded curves.

Alysha screamed as the first cut bit. It was Guinevere's turn to smother her sweetheart's cries with forceful kisses, her lips stifling her cries as the blows landed in their ordained stinging pattern of six across the quivering softness of her globes.

Mistress Domina finally lowered her cane to inspect her artistry. She caressed the heat of the raised welts with her hand. It was precision caning that left a set of six parallel stripes across each quivering bottom. The livid red welts would soon shade to a pleasing deep purple.

The girls stood immobile; an erotic Canova sculpture marbled in pain.

Mistress Domina clasped the two girls to her bosom and kissed their tearful faces.

'Now fuck!' she commanded. 'The pain will heighten the ecstasy of your orgasm. Finish what that Bullen bitch interrupted!'

Alysha smiled and bent to kiss Guinevere's perspiring breasts, coaxing their red nipples into excited erection. Her hand descended to caress Guinevere's taut tummy muscles, stole lasciviously lower to the copper curls of her fleece, fingered open her puffy love-lips to find it moistly ready. Guinevere gasped and thrust her pussy to meet the questing finger. The audience heard the unmistakable squelching sound of a cunt being lasciviously frigged before their eyes.

'Fuck me darling! Fuck me!' Guinevere's voice was husky with pent-up lust. She squirmed to the intrusive finger swirling inside her cunt, massaging her throbbing clit ever closer to its urgent orgasmic release

'I love you! I love you! I'm coming! I'm coming!'

Guinevere's knees buckled as her flooding climax took hold. She collapsed to the floor, clasping her lover's legs for support.

Alysha thrust her silky black muff into Guinevere's perspiring face. 'Suck me, Goddess! Suck me! Finish what that Bullen Bitch interrupted!'

She clutched Guinevere's head, pressing lips to her hungry cunt, rhythmically thrusting to the darting, loving, questing tongue slurping at her ruby pearl. A glow began to build, flamed suddenly and exploded in her belly as Guinevere's burrowing tongue flicked at her jewel to bring her finally to shuddering climax. She pumped her cunt, thrusting, grinding her love-lips onto Guinevere's heated face. Flexing and writhing in ecstatic, pain-induced delirium, her taut muscles quivered to the surging waves of orgasmic energy flooding through her body.

The storm was over, energy spent. Her shoulders slumped, head drooping for a moment in sated, perspiring exhaustion.

Alysha sucked her wet fingers, savouring Guinevere's fragrant cum juices. Then, raising her beloved from her knees, she kissed her lingeringly and led her from the salon.

There was silence followed by the sound of many orgasmic moans as Amazon fingers exposed the hidden treasure of their lover's hooded pearls.

Mistress Domina broke the spell. 'No wonder the Riding Mistress was jealous!'

Hardly Working
by Chloe Devlin

'I don't want to,' Wendy said petulantly. 'It's hot outside and those cartons are heavy. I don't feel like carting them into the storage room and unpacking them.'

Her boss, Jack Tremaine, stared at her in what had to be sheer amazement. After all, she was usually a model employee, but she hadn't gotten a lot of sleep last night. She'd been too busy fantasizing about Jack licking her as she made herself come over and over again. Besides it was hot and humid outside, a combination that made her very cranky.

'Are you refusing a direct order?' he asked sternly.

'Aw, Jack, don't make me,' she whined again. 'I told you. I don't want to. Besides, it's probably a bunch of crap that we don't need.'

'That's it.' Jack slammed his hand down on the countertop. He came out from behind the counter to the spinning rack display of condoms that she was restocking.

Before Wendy could blink, he had grabbed her wrists and cuffed them behind her, using a pair of their top-of-the-line metal cuffs. She gasped in shock. What on earth was he doing? What if a customer walked in?

'Now, this is the deal, Wendy,' he said. 'You've been a hard worker for several years. I enjoy having you work here, but I will not tolerate this sort of attitude. You have two choices. One, I will release the cuffs, you will collect your purse and you will never return to work here. Or two, you will accept discipline for your sass.'

Her heart skipped a beat as it started fluttering just a bit faster. 'What sort of discipline?'

'I think a baker's dozen on your bare behind should suffice.'

Her eyes widened. 'You mean a spanking?'

'That's exactly what I mean. You know you deserve it.'

Wendy couldn't believe her ears. She'd lusted after her boss since the day he'd hired her. But she'd never expected this. He was always friendly yet so businesslike.

'Well?' Jack asked impatiently. 'What's it to be? The first choice or the second?'

She stared at his face, his high cheekbones suffused with color. Arousal glittered in his eyes. She glanced downwards and saw a large bulge in his jeans and felt her pussy dampen with moisture. 'The second one,' she said.

He put a finger under her chin, lifting so that he could gaze into her eyes. 'Are you sure you know what you're getting into? If you say yes, I'm going to put out the closed sign and take you into the back office. You're going to take off all your clothes, including your jeans and panties and lay across my lap. Then I'm going to spank your ass thirteen times. And I won't hold back.'

She practically melted into a puddle of lust at his feet. How did he know that bare-bottom spankings turned her on? That when she was home, alone late at night, and she spread her legs and started to play with herself, that she dreamt of a strong, dominant man who would keep her in line and spank her until her ass burned with pleasure and turned bright red?

Trying to keep the excitement from showing on her face, she answered, 'I understand.'

'And you know that a good hard fucking always follows a good hard spanking.'

Lord, could she take any more without throwing herself at his feet and promising to be his slave for life? 'Yes, sir.'

A smile of satisfaction came over his features. 'Good. Then

let's begin. I've been waiting for this day for a long time.'

As promised, he flipped the sign to closed and locked the front door. His hand on her shoulder, he guided her towards the back workroom.

A long work table stood along one wall, open boxes of inventory that needed to be checked in and put out for sale on either end, a clear space in the middle. On the other side, Jack's desk stretched from wall to wall, paperwork scattered on top. He sank into his leather executive chair and leaned back, the springs creaking.

Wendy stood in the middle of the room, her hands still cuffed behind her, waiting for her instructions. Excitement poured through her veins, her heart nearly beating out of her chest. She could hardly stand still, shifting from foot to foot.

'Let me open those so you can strip.' Jack gestured with a cuff key dangling from his finger.

Wendy turned her back to him and he unlocked one wrist. With her hands free, she swung back around to face him, keeping her arms at her sides.

'Okay, strip,' he commanded. 'Everything.'

She swallowed; her mouth as dry as her fingers went to the snap and zipper of her jeans. It didn't take long to slide them off her legs. Then she removed her shirt, leaving herself clad only in a matching demi-cup bra and silk thong.

'I think I recognize that set,' he nodded to her lingerie. 'Used your employee discount, huh?'

'Yes, sir.' Somehow it seemed so natural to call him 'sir' in a respectful manner.

'Nice. Now take it off so I don't have to rip it.'

She removed the bra, her firm breasts standing upright, her large nipples starting to get hard. As she slid the thong down her legs and stepped out, Jack held out his hand. 'Give those here.'

The tiny thong was soaked with her juices and the scent of aroused female filled the air. Jack hung the scrap of silk from his lamp, the heat from the bulb warming the fabric and intensifying the scent.

'Are you ready, Wendy?' He sounded almost gentle, almost tender.

She licked her lips and nodded. 'Yes, sir. I am.'

He sat up, the chair springs squeaking again. 'Then come here and stretch yourself across my lap.'

She obeyed without any hesitation. Deep down inside, she craved this treatment, this punishment. And she knew Jack would never truly hurt her. Just make her butt burn enough to feel good.

'Hands behind your back,' he ordered, cuffing them together again when she did as he commanded.

Jack held his breath as his nubile employee draped herself over his thighs. His cock hardened even more, straining against his jeans. He never dreamed she'd actually go through with this, much less be totally turned on by the thought of getting her bare butt spanked. Yet here she was, offering those pale round cheeks to him.

Using his left hand to pull her cuffed wrists out of the way as well as to secure her on his lap, he caressed her creamy skin with his right, her cheeks quivering beneath his palm. He briefly dipped his fingers between her legs, feeling the moisture gathering there.

Without warning to her, he lifted his hand and brought it down on her bare flesh. Hard enough to sting his palm.

Wendy gasped, then said, 'One, sir.'

She continued to count the swats as he peppered both sides of her ass, turning the skin bright red. Heat flowed from her butt to his palm as he took a break and ran his hand over her reddened flesh before resuming.

She wriggled in his lap as he landed swats nine, ten and eleven, still counting each one aloud. When he landed number twelve, a cry escaped from Wendy, but she managed to gasp out the count.

'One more, Wendy,' he said sternly. 'And then what happens after your baker's dozen?'

'A good hard fucking, sir,' she said.

He reached between her legs again and found her pussy

totally wet and slick with her juices. 'Guess you're looking forward to that, aren't you?'

'Y-yes, sir,' she whimpered as he gently played with her labia, her juices coating his fingers.

'Good. Now ask me for the last one.'

'Oh, god,' she gasped. 'Please! One more. I can't wait to feel your hard cock in me.'

'As you wish,' he murmured and brought his open palm down, holding it firm against her hot skin.

She let out a cry and arched her back, shivers wracking her body. God, it was so hot, he thought. Watching her climax just from his spanking. Drops of moisture from her spasming pussy soaked through his jeans.

He gently rubbed her ass, letting her body shiver and shudder until the spasms started to lessen. Finally, she lay limply over his lap, still breathing heavily.

Wendy felt the last tremors of her orgasm shoot through her body. She'd never come just from a spanking before. Generally she needed a helping hand, usually her own, even after a guy had tanned her butt. But between the excitement from the swats on her flesh and the fact that it was Jack doing the spanking, she'd gone off like a firecracker.

Calloused hands grasped her shoulders, helping her to her feet. 'How was that, Wendy?'

'Um, good, sir,' she said.

'Not too soft? Not too hard?'

With her hands still cuffed behind her, she could feel the heat emanating from her ass as she pressed her wrists against herself. 'No, sir,' she replied. 'At the risk of sounding like Goldilocks, it was just right.'

'Good.' A smug smile graced Jack's face and then he pointed to the work table. 'Now it's time for the rest of your punishment. Go bend over there.'

Slightly unsteady on her feet, her legs still weak from her climax, she made her way to the work table. The height was just right with her in heels. As she leaned forward, the edge of the table caught her at her hips, and she let her chest rest against the shiny surface.

Her nipples hardened into tight buds, pressing against the cold hard tabletop. She shimmied her shoulders, letting them rub gently on the table, the pressure soothing the ache building in her chest.

She heard the creak of the chair as Jack stood. Even without turning her head, she knew he'd moved so that he was directly behind her, staring at her heated ass. She wondered if she had palm prints on her flesh, or if it was uniformly reddened all over.

Jack reached over and plucked something from one of the open boxes on the table. His denim covered cock brushed against the heat of her ass, sending a shiver of pleasure through her.

She felt a coolness drip onto her flesh at the top of the crack in her ass. Silky lubricant slid down between her hot cheeks, smoothing the way around her anus. One finger slid between her cheeks, tracing the path of the oil until he gently pushed the tip into her ass. She squealed softly, but pushed back against the pressure.

God, she couldn't wait to find out what he was going to do. It had been so long since she'd been fucked in the ass. Was that his plan?

He thrust his finger in and out of her asshole, spreading the slick lube all around – both inside and outside. 'You're going to wear a plug for me, Wendy,' he said. 'Not a big one, not a little one. But one that's just right.'

She squirmed, wanting to feel him filling her ass with something, anything, as long as it was bigger than his finger. 'Please, sir. I'm ready.'

He chuckled then slapped one cheek. 'I'll decide when you're ready.'

'Yes, sir.' It was so exciting to have everything taken out of her hands, to be at the whim of a hot, sexy guy who was determined to dominate her for both their pleasure.

He removed his finger and pressed the hard knob of the butt plug against the tiny opening. 'Push back,' he commanded. 'Relax and open up.'

She did as he ordered; feeling her anus flower open under the pressure until the widest part filled her insides and her muscles could contract around the smaller top of the plug.

'Good girl,' he complimented her. 'It looks nice and tight in there. Feel good?' He ran a couple of fingers down her ass crack again, pushing slightly against the plug.

'Uh, yes, sir,' she replied, her insides pulsing with desire. 'Just right.'

His big hands massaged her burning cheeks, squeezing the hot flesh with his fingers before soothing it with light caresses. 'You have an absolutely delectable ass, Wendy. Perfect for spanking and fucking.'

Before she could reply, he removed his hands. She heard the sound of his zipper opening and the soft rasp of his jeans as he took them off.

Her eyes widened slightly as he took an extra-extra-large condom from the stack right next to her head. His cock had felt pretty big under her belly when she'd been over his lap, but extra-*extra* big? She heard the snap of the condom as he rolled it on.

His hands patted the insides of her thighs. 'Wider,' he said, encouraging her to slide her feet further apart. Each inch that she shifted spread her wet labia, cool air wafting over her heated flesh.

Blunt fingers slid through the wetness, touching and caressing her open pussy. A sigh of pleasure escaped as he pushed one, then two fingers into her, calluses rasping against sensitized flesh. She tried to clamp her inner muscles around the invading digits, but he simply thrust them deeper, and then pulled them out.

'So wet, so ready for me.' He notched the plum-shaped head of his condom-covered cock at the entrance to her cunt, holding it there so it held her pussy lips apart.

'Please,' she whimpered, trying to shove her hips back. She couldn't wait to feel that huge shaft invading her body.

As if in answer to her plea, Jack gripped her butt cheeks,

his fingers digging into the tender flesh, then slowly, steadily slid his hard cock all the way in until his balls rested against her clit. The slow glide stretched her inner muscles with an erotic burn.

Wendy gloried in the feeling of being stuffed with Jack's cock in her pussy and a butt plug in her ass. She'd never felt so full, so excited, so close to coming. It wouldn't take much – just a thrust or two – to send her into orgasm.

'Yes, yes, that's it,' she gasped, feeling the broad head of his cock hit her cervix every time he shoved all the way in. Then the thick shaft dragged against tender flesh as he pulled almost all the way out before pumping in again.

Before he could finish the third thrust, her entire body tightened and a lightning bolt of pure sensation flashed through her body. She shivered with each pulse of her climax, unable to stop the spasms from shaking her body. Panting against the exquisite pinch of ecstasy, she nearly passed out from the pleasure.

As her body slowly came down off the peak of her orgasm, Jack leaned over her, his abdomen touching her hot ass, his chest pressing her cuffed hands against the small of her back. He lowered his body to hers, sliding his hands between her chest and the table, cupping her tits in his palms.

'Arch your back,' he ordered, massaging her breasts as she complied.

His fingers pinched her taut nipples, sending more zings of ecstasy from her tits to her clit. Then the sensations intensified again as he began to thrust in and out. He rolled her nipples between his fingertips, tightening the pressure on them. 'You like this? You like it when I pinch your nipples?'

Her heart thundering in her chest, her breath wheezing in and out, she couldn't answer for a minute as the pleasure began to overwhelm her. 'God, yes,' she moaned. 'Do it more. Pinch them harder.'

In response, he held on tighter and she felt the flames of ecstasy spiraling around her nipples, through her breasts and burning down to her stuffed pussy and ass. It had been so long since she'd been thoroughly dominated and fucked like this and she loved it! 'That's… it, sir.' The words escaped between each thrust into her. 'Please… I need to… come again.'

Releasing her throbbing nipples, he started pumping his hard cock faster, reaming her spasming pussy. She whimpered in disappointment at the loss of the pressure on her tits, but yelped with surprise when his large hand came down on one side of her hot ass. Then the other hand slapped the other side. With no rhyme or reason, he continued sporadically spanking her blushing ass.

The sting from his slaps, coupled with his increasing power of his shaft plunging deeper and deeper into her body, brought her to the edge of orgasm. 'Please, sir,' she begged. 'I need to come.'

'Wait for it,' he commanded. 'I'll let you come in a minute.'

She wiggled against the fullness invading her body, feeling the sensations growing stronger, knowing that she wouldn't be able to hold on much longer. Relaxing her muscles as much as she could, she let Jack piston his huge shaft in and out of her pussy.

Just when she thought she couldn't wait one more second, he brought both hands down on her spanked ass, his thumbs pressing on the butt plug. He thrust as deep into her body as possible and held his erection inside her. 'Now!' he shouted. 'Come for me now!'

She felt the warmth of his semen, even through the condom, as he spurted in orgasm. Her muscles clenched around his pulsing cock, milking every drop she could as her body shuddered and shook with her climax. Wordlessly, she cried out, feeling the sensations coursing through her body, increasing in intensity. She gasped for air, trying to keep her heart from beating right out of her chest.

Just as the spasms shaking her body began to lessen, Jack reached one hand beneath her, his fingers touching and rubbing her clit. Unadulterated ecstasy shot through her body, tightening every muscle, making her pant until she nearly passed out again.

Just as she thought she was going to faint, his fingers released her throbbing clit, letting her slowly down from the peak of her pleasure.

A tiny click sounded and her arms fell to her sides, her wrists released from the cuffs. She groaned as she brought her arms up. Turning her head to one side, she laid her head against her arms, not moving another muscle.

Jack leaned forward, enveloping her body as he brought his arms around her, cradling her against his chest. 'Are you okay?'

'I don't think I can move,' she said. 'I've never come that hard.'

'Not even when you've been spanked?'

She sighed, remembering several lovers who'd warmed her ass. 'Not even then. This was incredible.'

Nuzzling the soft skin beneath her ear, his breath warmed her lobe. 'You realize that our entire relationship has completely changed.'

She stiffened as his words rumbled in her ear. 'I know.'

'I know… what?'

She shivered with delight. 'I know, sir.'

'I'm not going to hesitate to spank your ass till it burns if you sass me again.'

There was only a slight hesitation before she said, 'I know, sir.'

'And I won't hesitate to fuck you in the ass if you misbehave.'

With his cock still in her pussy, the butt plug in her ass and his arms wrapped securely around her, she paused a moment. Finally, she turned her face farther back so that her lips practically touched his.

'I know, sir,' she replied, knowing that there was no going back, knowing that she didn't want to. 'I know.'

Colonial Times
by Mel. J. Fleming II

It was the year of 1773, in pastoral Boston countryside. The newly married Lord David and Lady Barrington had just arrived in their new large home, just outside the city limits. Nevia Barrington was a lady who desired all things be in perfect order for her husband, who was often out and about on King George's business in the Colonies.

The two new female servants, Mary and Sophia, were busy putting plates in the kitchen, while removal men put all the furniture in its proper order. The stable boys were currying and feeding the horses, all was busy as she gave directions.

Lord Barrington was a lovely but strict husband who believed in discipline when running his affairs. A former Commander in the Royal Navy, he was not against physical punishment, having had many seaman flogged on the gratings. In fact when he was engaged to Nevia, he had soundly spanked her several times on her sumptuously bare bottom when displeased with her behaviour.

There had been an occasion when she spoke ill of a lady at Royal Court, and he was told by one of his spying servants, whom he paid a fee to keep secret watch on her. Later that night, he made her take off her dress in a spare room, down to her bloomers. "Now, my darling, you had no business using a harsh tongue toward Lady Emerson. She was our hostess and you've grieved me deeply. Now you must learn a lesson in humility." He then sat in an armless chair, taking her over his lap, her bountiful bottom encased in her linen bloomers, placed in the proper spanking position. Taking his leather belt in his right hand, he doubled it, taking careful aim at her bottom.

Raising the belt, he suddenly let fly, and it made a loud snapping crack against her left

cheek! Nevia shrieked and kicked her legs, but she was tightly held in his grip. He struck her right cheek and her wails of pain and suffering began. The leather belt made cracking sounds against her bottom, becoming scorched from its impact.

"Oh please! I'm sorry! I'll never do it again! Please stop!"

However, unconvinced, David continued the whipping, lecturing poor Nevia on the virtues of the lady-like behaviour expected if they were to marry. The belt fell across her plump red bottom a dozen more times, before he finally stopped. He tossed the leather down, taking her in his arms, kissing her deeply, pulling down her bloomers, and massaging her bouncing sweaty backside.

He soon pulled her atop him, inhaling her beautiful breasts, like a suckling infant, as she cried from the horrible whipping she had received. However, while the tears ran down her face, she also felt sensual desire building inside as he disrobed while alternately kissing her lips and sucking and biting her copious breasts.

Soon, with them both naked, he pulled her on to him and she strode his immense penis as a rider would a prized stallion, moaning, gasping, sweat flowing down her face and shoulders. David was pulling her in a "back-forward" motion, making the mixture of pain and pleasure immeasurably joyful. Even though her bottom was aching from the whipping, after several minutes more, Nevia sank into his arms, smothering him with kisses, bathing David in hot, steamy sweat. Lying in each other's wetness, she promised to behave herself in a better manner, although later on he did give her several whippings, as a reminder.

Six months later, when affairs were well established, Lady

Nevia often took walks along the garden path into the forest to enjoy the natural surroundings. One Tuesday, though, when she was near the barn, she went to spy upon what she perceived to be a disturbance in the barn. She peeked in the doorway and was surprised to see Matthew, the senior stableman, spanking Mary the household maid! Mary was over Matthew's lap, her bare behind being beaten with his sandal. It was indeed a sight to see. Mary had a beautiful backside, curvy and plump, turning a bright pink under the skilful application of the old man's sandal! " I warned you what I'd do, girl, if I caught you in the barn without proper shoes on, didn't I?" growled Matthew. "I told you there were loose nails and things to hurt your feet, but you won't listen, will you?" Mary was wriggling, and sobbing like a spoiled child.

"This will learn ya to obey what I tell ya!"

Nevia, although indignant about the old man spanking Mary, was carried back to memories of how Lord David had whipped her own bottom on several occasions. She felt a strange warmth in her vagina, and began rubbing herself down below, to relieve what she felt. Her breathing became heavy, but she hushed herself, so as to not make any noise and disturb what was happening. Mary was squirming, twisting , arms flailing as Matthew's sandal continued its assault on her reddening bouncing cheeks. Matthew, after counting 50 strikes, stopped and let Mary up; she bolted away to the house, tears flowing down her face. Lady Nevia quickly left, heading for the forest, her mind swimming with a new sexual fantasy, almost losing track of where she was while walking. Her vagina was warm from the rubbing it had received while she was watching the punishment.

That Friday, while she was in the reading room, Lady Nevia heard a loud crash from the kitchen. Going to investigate, she saw an old family dish shattered on the floor. "What happened here?" she demanded.

"Please, Mam, it was my fault," Sophia whispered, with fear in her eyes. "It was an accident, I swear it."

"That plate was my grandmother's" shouted Nevia,

incensed at Sophia's apparent clumsiness."

"I'm sorry, Mam, I'll pay for it," pleaded Sophia."

"Oh yes, you'll pay alright, Sophia. You'll pay for it in a very special way, indeed! Go upstairs to your room now and wait for me there!"

Sophia, her face filled with fear, ran to her room, wondering what her ladyship would do. After a few minutes Nevia entered the room with a freshly cut birch switch. "Sophia, I can't believe you could be that damn clumsy. You've been in my family's service since your mother had you. You know better. Now lower your dress to the underskirt, and step out of it!" Sophia quickly did as directed. "Now turn around, bare your bottom and bend forward, over the bed, placing your hands on it." Sophia slowly turned and bent over the bed. Nevia then placed the switch over her small bared bottom. "I hope you learn a lesson from this, Sophia," said Nevia."

She raised the frightening straight switch, and brought it forcefully down upon Sophia's smooth, round bottom! "OW, my lady." The switch fell quickly three more times.

"OOWWWWW ,AAAWWWW," Sophia screamed out, tears running from her eyes in rivers. "Please, my lady, have pity!"

Nevia continued the switching, while poor Sophia cried out for forgiveness! Red lines formed all over Sophia's backside as she gestured wildly, but stayed bent over the bed! After four dozen swipes, Nevia finally ceased, and gave Sophia a stern lecture and warning concerning her duties. "Now go and assist Mary with supper."

That evening when Lord David was reading, after a wonderful meal, he noticed that Sophia was not her usually happy self. Nevia was instructing Mary in the kitchen. "Sophie, my dear, what's wrong with you today? Has someone died?" inquired his Lordship.

"Nay, my Lord, I broke one of your old plates, and was punished."

Lord David seemed puzzled.

"Just what do you mean by 'punished'?"

"My Lady Nevia gave me what for across me bum with a right good switch, from the birch tree, she did," replied the maid.

"Oh, did she now?" mused his Lordship. He called out; "Nevia, my dear! Please come here, now! I want a word!"

Nevia appeared quickly. "Yes, my darling?"

David gave her a curious look. "What's this I hear that you switched Sophie for a broken plate? And with a birch switch, without my permission?"

Nevia looked astounded "I need your permission to discipline the servants?"

"Yes my dear, you do. I'm the one who pays their salaries, therefore I'm the one who decides their deductions and punishments."

Nevia now had a frightened look on her face. *Oh, no, now I've really done it to myself*, she thought. "Ahhh, I'm sorry my love, I didn't think you'd disapprove, I mean, I meant no harm."

David looked at Nevia, whose hands were shaking. "Well, my dear we shall have to have a chat upstairs about this, now won't we? Go to our room immediately, if you please, and you know what to do."

Nevia went upstairs and upon entering the room quickly removed her dress, to her bloomers. She knew full well what was coming. Soon her eyes began to well up with tears, as she anticipated what was to happen. After what seemed an eternity her husband entered the room ... with a new-cut birch switch! Nevia was terrified beyond belief. David had only to motion with his hands as he sat in a plush chair. "So ... you gave Sophie 4 dozen with this eh? Well my dear you shall also receive the same, but first, I think, a good spanking."

David took Nevia over his lap, and this time lowered her bloomers, revealing those lusciously bountiful, plump, and bouncy bottom cheeks. He placed his right hand in the centre, then almost immediately began an extremely sound spanking on her naked backside.

"OWWW!, screamed her ladyship as the whacks fell again and again, quickly pinkening her backside. Nevia kicked, bucked, and twisted like a bucking horse, however David's hand never failed to find its target. Her bottom was becoming unbearably hot, scorching, as if she was a slave being branded. Each spank made it worse, as David spanked her with vigour.

Nevia's bottom was bouncing, reddening and wriggling fervently with each smack. Even unbearable as the pain was, though, she knew in her heart he was doing this because of his love for her. That was her only comfort during the dreadful ordeal. She could only hope that he would stop soon. Then she realised the switch would be next!

When David ended the spanking, he picked up his sobbing wife and had her bend on the bed, as Sophia had done for her earlier. He flicked the switch onto Nevia's bottom before increasing the speed and intensity of the strokes. The switch made whirring sounds through the air, as Nevia screamed with each delivery.

Outside the door, listening, Mary and Sophia were silently giggling, like nervous schoolgirls, as her ladyship wailed with each stroke.

"My God is she getting it, or what?" said Mary.

David counted the four dozen, then made his wife lie face down on the bed, as her sobbing could be heard throughout the house. He then called for Sophia to bring him a pomade for his wife.

"I think you've learned the lesson, my dearest, his lordship said as he hugged his blubbering wife, massaging the pomade into her blistered, deeply reddened bottom.

As much as she was in frightful pain, Nevia knew that a passionate session of lovemaking was soon to come. And in that knowledge, she took comfort.

Xcite Dating – turning fiction into reality!

Xcite Books offer fabulous fantasy-filled fiction. Our unique dating service helps you find that special person who'll turn your fantasies into reality!

You can register for FREE and search the site completely anonymously right away – and it's completely safe, secure and confidential.

www.xcitedating.com

Interested in spanking?

Spanking is our most popular theme so we have set up a unique spanking site where you can meet new friends and partners who share your interest.

www.xcitespanking.com

The Education of Victoria
A novel by Angela Meadows

Lessons in love and a whole lot more are in store in this saucy romp set in a European finishing school for young ladies.

Packed off to a continental finishing school, 16-year-old Victoria thinks she will be taught how to be a dutiful wife for a gentleman. But she soon discovers that she has a lot to learn in the arts of pleasure at the Venus School for Young Ladies.

There she encounters the strictness of Principal Madame Thackeray and her team of tutors. Under their guidance she learns the finer arts of sexual pleasure and discovers that there are plenty of fellow students and staff willing to share their carnal knowledge with this sweet young English rose.

On returning to England, she finds her father in financial difficulty and must turn her newfound education to good use to survive.

£7.99 ISBN 9781906373696

The True Confessions of a London Spank Daddy

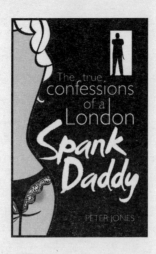

Discover an underworld of sex, spanking and submission. A world where high-powered executives and cuddly mums go to be spanked, caned and disciplined.

In this powerful and compelling book Peter Jones reveals how his fetish was kindled by corporal punishment while still at school and how he struggled to contain it. Eventually, he discovered he was far from alone in London's vibrant, active sex scene.

Chapter by chapter he reveals his clients' stories as he turns their fantasies into reality. The writing is powerful, the stories graphic and compelling.

Discover an unknown world...

£7.99 ISBN 9781906373320

The Xcite Guide to Sexy Fun
by Aishling Morgan

This book is about pleasure; joyful, liberated, sexual pleasure.

User-friendly – it's designed for the curious amateur. It's about pleasures that go beyond what most people are used to, and beyond what is generally accepted as mainstream, not just sex, but naughty sex, the kind of sex that involves more leather than lace, more kink than kissing, that involves bound wrists and smacked bottoms and perhaps even the occasional jugful of custard!

£9.99 ISBN 9781906373863